CW01642520

He lifted her chin and looked down at her. 'I've had a wonderful evening, Claire. I want you to know that this past month has been one of the happiest times of my life.'

She waited to hear the rest, wondering why it sounded awfully like a dismissal.

'And of course we'll carry on seeing each other, though it's not going to be easy—with your hours and my being on call so much.'

'I know.' She gazed at Luke's mesmeric eyes, so grey tonight, wanting to lock the memory of them firmly away for ever.

'I want you to know . . .' his voice faltered a little. 'You mean so much to me, Claire, but . . .'

'Luke . . .'

He shushed her gently. 'Listen, my darling. You're still so very young. You've your whole life in front of you, and it *has* only been a month. We must neither of us make any promises which we may not be able to keep. Do you understand?'

Claire nodded numbly.

Sharon Wirdnam has been a waitress, a photographer and a cook. She then trained as a nurse and medical secretary and found that she enjoyed working in a caring environment. She decided that one day she would write about romance against the dramatic backdrop of hospital life.

She was encouraged to write by her doctor husband after the birth of their two children, and much of her medical information comes from him, and from friends.

She lives in Surrey, where her husband is a GP. *To Break a Doctor's Heart* is her second Doctor Nurse Romance; the first was *Nurse in the Outback*.

TO BREAK A DOCTOR'S HEART

BY

SHARON WIRDNAM

MILLS & BOON LIMITED
ETON HOUSE 18-24 PARADISE ROAD
RICHMOND SURREY TW9 1SR

First published in Great Britain 1989
by Mills & Boon Limited

This edition 1989

ISBN 0 263 76384 6

Set in English Times 11 on 12 pt.
03 – 8904 – 48474

Typeset in Great Britain by JCL Graphics, Bristol

Made and Printed in Great Britain

dedication For Don, Joan and Eileen

CHAPTER ONE

HER ROOM in the Nurses' Home was small and cramped. She still found it hard to believe she was where she was; sometimes she would hover in the warm half-world between sleeping and waking, blinking in surprise when eventually her eyes opened.

The walls had once—unbelievably—been painted in a dark olive green emulsion, she knew this because great murky patches showed through the present light green colour, which was peeling off in handfuls. But Claire didn't care, the gloomy surroundings didn't matter—even they could not quell the enthusiasm which had been bubbling up inside her for weeks now and was threatening to spill over at any time. As she pinned the brand new fob watch on to her uniform, the sunlight caught the glass and it flashed brilliantly—a symbol of the bright new future that lay ahead of her.

She rubbed her finger along the inside of the unfamiliar stiff, starched collar and surveyed her image in the mirror, really starting to believe for the first time that she was now Student Nurse Scott. The girl who stared back at her was no longer the leggy, successful top model, whose wide professional smile for the camera concealed a growing awareness of her shallow life-style, but one of the general public's very own 'angels'.

Her copper curls—once her most bankable trademark—had been tied and tamed, and now only their colour appeared riotous beneath the white linen cap. She wore a white starched apron over the pale blue striped uniform dress, and the white belt which covered her waist marked her out as one of the Introductory Block, or 'new girls' as they were known at St Anthony's. The fine black stockings and neat shoes accentuated her slim ankles and shapely legs. She had been in the School of Nursing wearing mufti for almost twelve weeks, but today was to be her first on the wards proper.

She could hear echoing sounds of laughter and chattering outside her room, presumably in the direction of the canteen. She had just drunk a cup of tea which she had made in her room earlier—she knew that they served a variety of breakfasts from as early as six a.m., but she felt far too excited to eat anything.

She glanced at her fob watch for the twentieth time. She still had over ten minutes before she should start out for Belton Ward, and just for a moment she allowed herself to think of him. Luke Hayward. She would not be standing in a nurse's uniform if it were not for him. Her whole life had changed direction and Luke Hayward had been the catalyst, and she knew about him—what?

Practically nothing really, she mused as she gave the regulation black shoes a final flick with a cloth. Except that he had seemed dedicated to his work, and very caring. And that he had intelligent grey-green eyes, firm lips, a strong jaw and hair which was a curious mixture of golden and brown. Which was little more than she knew when she had first seen him from across the other side of a crowded restaurant . . .

It had been a fashionable fish restaurant in North London and he had been sitting with three women, including a slim woman with pale hair who had been smiling up at him lazily. Claire had been dining with Simon Saunders—he had been asking her out for months and eventually she had agreed to have supper with him.

She had been aware that her colleagues would have been envious if they had known that she was out with the tall, shaggy-haired photographer, but she had been bored by his gossipy comments about the other models he worked with. It seemed that he was as superficial as most of the other people she usually hung around with.

Claire had looked up, vainly trying to stifle a yawn, when she had found herelf staring into a pair of very amused grey-green eyes, and he had raised his glass to her and smiled, with a kind of elegant old-world courtesy which had charmed her, and she had blushed.

That had been all, but the questioning look in those eyes had planted a seed of doubt in her mind, causing her to begin to analyse the quality of her whole lifestyle—never realising that at their next meeting he was to help her change it irrevocably.

She sighed as she gathered up the scarlet-lined

woollen cloak and a slight frown appeared between the dark brows which framed slanting eyes of hyacinth blue. She was longing to see him again, longing to tell him that she had thrown caution to the wind and had taken his advice.

She took a final glance around the room as she opened the door—it really *was* tiny; the expression 'no room to swing a cat' might have been invented for the nurses' accommodation at St Anthony's Hospital!

A narrow bed and rather scratched bedside locker had somehow been squeezed in. In the corner of the window stood a large old-fashioned white enamel wash-basin. At least the view made up for it—the rather Gothic architecture of Hampstead contrasted dramatically with the unexpectedly wild sweep of green which was Hampstead Heath.

It had been drummed into the nurses how lucky they were to be training in North London, since apparently at another famous London hospital, the Nurses' Home backed on to a very large prison!

Mrs Haynes, her tutor, had explained that they liked the Introductory Block to live in the Nurses' Home for the first twelve weeks—partly to get to know each other and partly to become fully integrated into hospital life.

'I have no objection to your living out in a flat after that,' she had told Claire in her first week. 'Although I do think that you might find it a bit of a trek to get here on time from Notting Hill, especially on an early duty. Why not move closer?'

Claire had taken her at her word, had put her old flat on the market, sold it almost immediately, and was due to move into her new flat in Primrose Hill that weekend, only a couple of miles from St Anthony's.

She set off for the main hospital building, which was a short walk away. Today was an important day. Today, as Mrs Haynes had joked to the class, they were about to be let loose on the patients! They were each to spend the Friday morning on their allotted wards, as a kind of gentle grounding before they started on the wards full-time next week.

Claire was to report to Sister Thompson on Belton Ward at seven-thirty a.m. She felt excited yet slightly apprehensive as she carefully smoothed her spare apron over her arm, trying not to crease it.

Mrs Haynes had warned them that the first day on a new ward was often a baptism of fire. 'Some are smitten, others take longer to like it, while some can't stand it and come straight to my office with their notice written out.'

Claire hoped fervently that she wouldn't be amongst the last group. She had enjoyed her time in the School of Nursing tremendously, but the wards were a different story completely, with different demands. She prayed that she would find them a challenge rather than daunting.

At least in class she had already found herself a friend. She had found herself sitting next to a small, dark girl with an infectious grin, called Mary

Wells. The two girls had shared an immediate bond as they had both worked at other jobs before starting nursing. The other twenty-four in the class had all come straight from school, and to Claire they seemed much younger.

As she walked towards Belton, she could see huge silver trolleys being trundled down the main corridor by the catering staff, with hot breakfasts on their way to each of the wards.

She had been a student nurse for eleven and a half weeks, but in all that time she had not had the opportunity to speak to Luke Hayward. The School of Nursing was quite separate from the main hospital building, and she had never seen him at lunchtime in the canteen.

She could of course have had him bleeped and arranged to meet him, but what on earth would she say? She could hardly blurt out, 'Hello, Luke—it's Claire Scott. I'm the girl you saw in the restaurant and then we met briefly in Casualty—remember? And you gave me some advice and I took it, and here I am. Oh, and by the way, I feel I can trust you more than anyone I've ever met, even though I hardly know you.' A small smile crossed her lips as she tried to imagine his reaction to such an outburst.

In fact, she had seen him only once since she'd been at the hospital, and that had been from a distance. A group from her set were being shown around the Pharmacy and were just about to leave, when suddenly about five doctors all tore past the door, their bleeps shrilling in a relentless high-pitched tone.

And one of them was Luke, Claire had noted dispassionately.

At that moment a voice on the tannoy began repeating, 'Cardiac emergency—Casualty. Cardiac emergency—Casualty!'

A hush had fallen over the chattering group of student nurses, and the pharmacist had quietly explained that the Medical Registrar, the anaesthetist and any spare doctors would be needed to try to resuscitate a patient whose heart had stopped.

Claire had stood back with the others and watched them retreat to the end of the long, wide corridor. She had thought she detected a murmur of approval as he dashed past them, running like an athlete, a shaft of sunlight turning his hair into molten gold, his face tense with concentration.

She hadn't mentioned him to anyone, not even to Mary, but then again—what could she possibly say about him? That she had seen him once in a restaurant, and had been besotted by him, like a schoolgirl? Or that she'd seen him almost in a professional capacity, when he had gently eased her out of shock that day? And that she'd told a complete stranger secrets close to her heart?

She wondered what Mary would say if she knew that if it hadn't been for Luke Hayward's casual suggestion, coming as it did like a bolt out of the blue, she wouldn't have been standing here in her brand new uniform, but would probably have been yawning her way through yet another photo session.

As she passed the Pharmacy, down the same wide corridor, she reflected on how much she had enjoyed the Introductory Block, and how she had taken to studying again like a duck to water.

Contrary to what her mother had told her, she had positively thrived under all the new intellectual demands. The uninterested pale student of her schooldays, still reeling from her parents' divorce, had blossomed into an eager consumer of all this new, scientific knowledge. She had found the anatomy and physiology fascinating—it was like the most marvellous detective story she had ever read, to discover how the human body worked. Mrs Haynes was an enthusiastic teacher, and covered some basic bio-chemistry and pathology in her lectures.

'It isn't strictly necessary for a nurse to know any of the chemical pathologies. But no knowledge is ever wasted, and the broader your education, then the better nurse you'll be for it,' she had told them.

Claire walked briskly up the stairs to the first floor corridor, her new black shoes shining brightly. At the ward entrance she stood peering around, feeling for a moment very young and inexperienced, and then she spotted a sign saying 'Sister's Office' and, clearing her throat nervously, she tapped softly on the door.

A voice called out 'Come in' and she stepped inside.

The Ward Sister, distinguishable by her dark navy dress and elaborately frilled cap, sat at her desk, a coffee cup in front of her and a set of notes by her hand. She looked to be in her late thirties, was very plump, and had the kindest face that Claire had ever seen.

'Hello there,' she said. 'Nurse Scott, isn't it?'

Claire nodded. 'Yes, Sister.'

'Good! Nice and early, that's what I like to see. Now, I'm just about to get the night report from Sister, so I'll get Nurse Hunter to show you where to hang your cloak, and what's where, and then you can all come in for report after you've given out the breakfasts. Nurse!' she called in a loud voice from the door, and a nurse as tall as Claire appeared. She wore her thick black hair tied back in a bun and looked at Sister inquisitively.

'Show Student Nurse Scott where to hang her cloak and around the ward, will you, Hunter?'

'Yes, Sister. Follow me.'

Claire trotted off obediently behind her. The blue belt she wore identified her as a third-year.

'This,' announced Nurse Hunter, 'is Belton Ward.'

It was an old-fashioned Nightingale ward in design, with rows of beds on either side of a central aisle. At the far end was the patients' day-room and the four bathrooms. Sister's office, the clinic-room, doctors' office, kitchen and sluice were nearest the ward entrance.

'You'll soon get to know where everything is,' the older nurse advised Claire. 'Come on, we'd better get a move on.'

Then began the busiest morning that Claire had

ever known. She scarcely had time to draw breath as they tipped cornflakes into bowls, poured teas and dolloped spoonfuls of marmalade on to the sides of plates. And all the time Nurse Hunter kept up an astonishingly fluent commentary which had Claire's mind in a spin, wondering if she would be able to remember any of it.

'That's the sluice over there, but you don't keep going in and out of there at mealtimes, not unless you absolutely have to—or Sister'll have your guts for garters. Morning, Mr Atkins! Pleased to be going home, are you? Mr Atkins has been with us nearly three months, haven't you, Mr Atkins?' she asked him cheerfully.

'Yes, Nurse. Looked after me good and proper, you 'ave.'

Nurse Hunter beamed and piled two heaped teaspoonfuls of sugar into his tea. 'Always try and learn whether your patient has any special dietary needs,' she confided. 'I'll never forget on my first ward when I asked a diabetic patient if he wanted sugar!' She burst into laughter at the memory, the smile lighting up her rather sallow face.

After they had finished serving out the breakfasts, she showed Claire where the clinic-room was. 'That's where we draw up injections and get out dressing trolleys ready,' she explained. 'And never take a dirty dressing trolley back in until you've cleaned it down properly, or Sister'll be after you!'

Sister sounded formidable, thought Claire, although Nurse Hunter seemed to speak of her quite affectionately.

'Let's just strip this bed before report,' she stopped by a rumpled empty bed. 'Mr Fellowes is always first into the bathroom. Then he goes down to the day-room for a smoke.'

Claire looked surprised. 'Are they allowed to smoke, then?'

The other girl pulled a face. 'Not really, but some of the old boys have smoked for so long that they just can't give it up. Sister lets them have one or two if they're desperate.'

So the practice didn't always follow the theory, thought Claire as she and Nurse Hunter rhythmically folded each sheet and blanket into three and then turned the bottom sheet over and straightened it. Mrs Haynes would be horrified to think that smoking was allowed!

Sister Thompson appeared at the door of her office, beaming widely down the ward.

'Morning, gentlemen,' she cried.

'Morning, Sister!' they chorused back at her.

'Right, girls. Into my office for report, please.'

'What's your first name?' hissed Nurse Hunter as they trooped into Sister's office behind two yellow-belted second-year nurses.

'Claire. What's yours?'

'It's Anna—but christian names aren't allowed on the wards. Don't forget!'

Claire nodded and sat down next to Anna Hunter, her pen and notebook in her hand, thinking what an awful lot of rules there were to remember.

Sister then began to run through a list of the patients, their age, diagnosis and treatment and whether there had been any change in their condition during the night.

'You won't understand much to begin with,' she told Claire kindly. 'But don't worry—by the time you leave us, you'll be telling me what to do!'

She let out a great thundering guffaw at this remark and the other nurses, including Claire, laughed politely, though she could never imagine knowing a fraction of the conditions which had been mentioned already. Pleural effusion; diabetic keto-acidosis; congestive cardiac failure; unexplained splenomegaly and purpura—the list seemed endless, and she wasn't even sure that she had spelt them properly!

It was all very well learning the twelve cranial nerves in class by reciting a complicated rhyme:

'On old Olympus' towering tops
A fierce and glowering vulture always hops.'

But learning about real diseases was going to prove a lot more difficult.

She realised that Sister was speaking to her.

'I'd like you to do a blanket bath on a patient who was admitted during the night with acute bronchitis. He's a bit washed out this morning, poor fellow.' She smiled at Claire. 'If you get stuck—just ask. Don't be shy. Things are always a bit hectic here, especially first thing in the morning, and I have to get ready for Dr Stellingworth's ward round. But later on I'll show you round properly.

'Right then, let me introduce you to your patient.'

She walked swiftly to the second nearest bed to her office. A very thin, anxious-looking man, his face partially obscured by a green oxygen mask, lay gasping against a great heap of pillows.

'Good morning, Mr Lucas,' said Sister quietly, bending down to talk to him. 'I've brought one of our new nurses along. This is Nurse Scott and she's going to give you a bed bath. Then Dr Stellingworth will be coming to see you. All right?'

He gave her the glimmer of a smile. Claire gulped nervously. He looked terribly ill, and what was she supposed to do about his oxygen mask while she was washing his face?

As if sensing her hesitation, Sister Thompson said softly:

'Don't worry—Mr Lucas is able to do without his mask for short periods. I'd really liked to have stayed and helped you with him, but we're so desperately short-staffed this week. Come with me and I'll show you where we keep the bowls.'

Claire filled a plastic bowl with warm water and drew the curtains around the cubicle, as she had been taught by Mrs Haynes.

It was certainly easier to bath the life-sized plastic doll in the School of Nursing than a real person, she thought, as she gently patted her patient's face dry. She sensed that Mr Lucas was too breathless to want to chat, so she went about her work gently and silently. She changed the water in the bowl several times, and when she had finished washing him Sister came in and helped change his pyjamas and make the bed.

'I'd like you to go to coffee with Nurse Hunter when you've finished here,' said Sister.

Claire nodded—she was dying for a cup of coffee, but already she felt twice as confident as she had done when she'd walked on to the ward that morning. She had given her first blanket bath and the patient had come through unscathed!

It was while she was finishing off Mr Lucas's chin with the electric shaver that she heard a male voice echoing outside the cubicle.

'Come on, Sister. I haven't got time to dawdle while you fuss around powdering your nose!'

'That'll be the day,' retorted Sister goodhumouredly, pulling back the curtain. 'You can go to coffee now, Nurse Scott. Dr Stellingworth is waiting to examine Mr Lucas.'

Luke Hayward, standing by the notes trolley with his house officer, senior house officer and a whole clutch of medical students, heard the name and started involuntarily. Surely it couldn't be the same Scott?

But then he saw her, coming out of the cubicle, looking like a sweet, seductive angel, her eyes sparkling like jewels and her cheeks pink from her exertions. A single red-gold curl lay on her cheek like a sculpture. She had done it—she had taken his advice!

Claire, carrying a basin full of soapy water, was mortified to see Luke Hayward standing there, surrounded by a crowd of other doctors, and her colour heightened even more.

She walked towards the sluice-room and you could have heard a pin drop. Then the silence was broken by Dr Stellingworth demanding, 'Where's the admitting houseman who wrote these appalling notes?' He strode behind the curtains, followed by a terrified-looking young doctor.

Pulling his stethoscope out of his white coat, Luke watched out of the corner of his eye as she and another nurse collected their cloaks and left the ward. He'd seen literally thousands of girls in uniform over the years, but he had never seen anyone wear it quite like Claire.

Bill Dixon, his SHO, also stood there, his eyes frankly appraising. He made a soft sound. 'Wow!' he said. 'It looks like the décor of the ward has been a hundred per cent improved!'

'I see that there's been no peak flow reading done on Mr Lucas since the time of his admission,' interrupted Luke coldly.

'I'm sorry,' the other replied, slightly taken aback. 'I've done two, actually—it's just that I haven't written them in the notes yet.'

'Really, Bill,' said Luke sarcastically. 'If you used just one quarter of the enthusiasm in your work that you display whenever a pretty nurse is around, then you'd be a far better doctor, in my opinion.'

Scowling, he pushed back the curtains to join the consultant and Bill Dixon was left standing there, feeling rather bewildered. It was not like his boss to be so snappy. They'd both often commented on good-looking nurses before. He raised his eyebrows at one of the medical students who had overheard the proceedings and grimaced, then began to write the peak flow results down.

Forcing himself to concentrate on a discussion with Dr Stellingworth about the various options open for treating Mr Lucas, Luke was himself surprised at his behaviour. Bill hadn't acted so appallingly, had he? Of course he hadn't. But he wanted to protect the girl from the men like Bill who would all be flocking round her like wasps round a jamjar. He felt responsible for her, that was all. If it hadn't been for his suggestion, then she most probably would never have come here to St Anthony's.

She was so heartbreakingly young—far too young for him. And far too young for every stag of a houseman to be pursuing her, he thought grimly.

Nevertheless, when the consultant's round finished and they all adjourned to Sister's office for coffee, he found himself loitering by the notice board until he found the nurses' off-duty list and could see when she would be there next.

CHAPTER TWO

AND ALL Claire could think about as she and Anna pushed open the ward doors was that day on Primrose Hill . . . a cold sunny March morning which was to change her life.

She remembered deciding to travel to North London for a change—she wanted to pay a visit to a little shop she knew in Primrose Hill. It was in a small parade just yards from Regent's Park Zoo and sold delicate antique lace and dresses. It was not far from the restaurant which Simon had taken her to a fortnight earlier, where she had seen the man with the enigmatic eyes, whose one brief glance had seemed to startle her out of her boredom and complacency.

Was that why she had come here today? Was she perhaps hoping to see him again? an inner voice asked her. But she told the voice to be quiet; London was a huge city and she would probably never see him again.

She took a bus all the way, and it was packed with people, but once beyond Marble Arch the crowds thinned away and she was able to sit and think in peace.

There had been a letter from her mother that morning, gaily telling her that she was planning an extended trip to America with her new husband.

Claire couldn't help but give a small sigh. She had tried so hard to like Ian McGregor, tried for her mother's sake as well as his. But she couldn't shake off her initial impression that he was a poor replacement for her father. Perhaps it was fortuitous, then, that the new husband should have taken his wife to live in New Zealand, and that all three were to be spared the confirmation of an uneasy relationship.

The bus stopped and Claire stepped out on to the pavement just below the Hill itself. It was a perfect spring morning, with a sky the colour of a bird's egg. Although the sun shone, the air was sharp and tangy and the first purple and white crocuses were beginning to peep out from beneath the bases of the trees.

She hoped that a shopping trip and a change of scene might dispel some of the niggling gloom which had recently threatened to envelop her. And yet there was no real reason for despondency—she was nineteen years old, a successful model earning a very creditable salary, with her own flat in the centre of London. What more could she possibly want?

She didn't know, but she felt as though a better life could be within her reach, if only she knew how to go about grasping it.

Success had come to her early—she had been living on her own since she was sixteen, and she had had to learn to protect herself from the men who seemed hell-bent on seduction. She had been teased for being standoffish by the wine-swilling account executives and the braying immature city stockbrokers whom she met. But their wild, drunken parties had held not the slightest attraction for her—she preferred solitary evenings in front of the television to the forced jollity of the crowd's 'high jinks'.

She gave her shoulders a little shake, and mentally chided herself. It was pointless feeling sorry for herself—it was a glorious spring morning, she had a free day ahead of her, and she was going to jolly well make the most of it!

She spent an enjoyable hour looking through the racks of dresses, and eventually settled on a diaphanous creation in the palest of pink silk tulle. The skirt fell in many layers to just above the ankle and the top layer was edged with a delicate border of embroidered flowers.

It was far more than she had wanted to pay, but it was ages since she had bought anything, and besides, she felt like treating herself. She paid by cheque and, thanking the young owner, took her carrier bag and went outside.

She looked at her watch. It was getting on for midday. Maybe she should stroll on the Hill for a while and then look for somewhere to lunch.

As she opened the gates which led on to Primrose Hill, the first subtle wakenings of spring reminded her of her holiday in Greece, and her blood quickened slightly. She had stopped going to the clubs and parties which were simply a hot, smoky crush, and which she hadn't been enjoying at all, and she felt much better for it.

Simon had been phoning her all week, but she had told him that she intended to live a quiet existence for the time being, and he had told her to 'give him a bell' when she felt like company again.

She had told her agent to lessen up on her bookings and had sent for several brochures from her local night school, thinking that she might take up painting. It might not completely solve her discontentment, she thought, but at least it might take her mind off it.

She walked briskly up to the summit of the hill, swinging her white and silver carrier bag as she did so. Her curls blew wildly around her head, the bright sunshine lighting them from behind so that they blazed red-gold, like a furnace.

When Claire reached the top of the hill, she stood there, breathing deeply and marvelling in the superb panoramic view across London. She could see the tall column of the Post Office Tower in the distance, and in the foreground the bizarre shrouded shape of the Zoo's aviary.

She could see a man walking up towards her, not sticking to the path, but walking between the quaint little lamp-posts. He was moving rather oddly, she noticed. Even from a couple of hundred yards away, she could see that his face was red and glistening with sweat, and as she watched his gait became even more unsteady.

As he approached, she could hear the laboured sound of his breathing. He was pulling at his tie and then, to her absolute horror, she watched him fall to the ground, gasping, and clutching at his chest.

For a moment she remained frozen and immobile, and then she sprang into action. She had reached him in a few seconds, and she saw that his face was almost grey, and his lips tinged with blue.

'Help me, please help me . . .' The words died on his lips.

Claire looked around wildly. She saw a teenager on a bike, a dog running behind him.

'Help!' she screamed. 'Go and ring for an ambulance. Quickly!'

To her relief he didn't hesitate, but sped down the hill at a breakneck pace.

Claire felt utterly, utterly helpless. She looked down at the man. At least he was still breathing, although with a horrible low, moaning sound which terrified her.

She didn't have a clue what to do; she had never even done so much as a first aid course at school. She remembered that the man had been tugging at his collar, and so she undid the two top buttons and loosened it. He had a handkerchief in his top pocket, and she gently removed it and wiped away the sweat from his face.

'What's your name?' she asked, taking his hand in hers.

'Phillips—Alex Phillips,' he whispered.

'Well, try not to worry, Mr Phillips,' she told him, with more confidence than she felt. 'The ambulance will be here soon.'

He squeezed her hand gratefully and Claire sat

there praying that the ambulance *would* get there soon.

She heard the siren from several streets away and then she saw the ambulance speeding towards them. It skidded to a halt outside the railings, the blue light on the roof spinning round and round like a propeller. She saw the young boy run up to the vehicle and point in her direction, and then the two ambulance men were pulling the stretcher from the back and running up the hill towards them.

When they reached her, one of them put two fingers on the man's neck.

'Weak pulse,' he said briefly. 'All right, miss, we'll just get him on the stretcher now.'

Claire stood back as they gently rolled him on to the stretcher, releasing his hand as she did so. His eyes flickered open briefly and he looked up at her.

'Stay with me,' he muttered. 'Please stay.'

She looked questioningly at them. One of them shrugged.

'That's OK. You can come, but you'll have to step on it.'

Forgetting her shopping, she ran behind them, back down the hill. They carefully lifted the stretcher into the back of the ambulance and Claire joined one of the crew in the back, while the other ran round to the cab, jumped in and started the engine.

She watched as the ambulanceman attached a monitor to the man's chest, and a thin luminous green light began to track across a small screen like a television.

'Sinus rhythm—that's good,' he said, to no one in particular. 'But ST elevation, though.'

He seemed to have forgotten who Claire was, he was speaking to her almost as though she were a nurse, although he might as well have been speaking in Greek, for all that she understood.

Th man's eyes flickered open again. He was middle-aged, but a slim, fit-looking middle-aged. She didn't think that men like that had heart attacks. His thick hair was frosted with silver. It could have been her father lying there, she thought, then tried to block out the thought immediately.

He glanced over to where she sat on the edge of the opposite stretcher and gave her a weak smile. Claire smiled back as encouragingly as she could. Meanwhile the ambulance was tearing through the streets, only switching on the shrill, terrifying blare of the siren if they came to traffic jams or red lights.

Through the darkened glass at the back she could see that they were going up Haverstock Hill, and there, at last, on the right-hand side, was the entrance to the hospital.

They stopped by some double doors, where they seemed to have been expected, because they flew open immediately and two nurses and a doctor came running out to meet them.

The doctor leapt up the three steps in one, and Claire gave a small gasp. It was the man from the restaurant!

She saw the light of recognition in his eyes, and then he was turning to the patient, his fingers feeling for a pulse, his eyes glued to the small screen, watching the line of the monitor as it rhythmically rose and fell, looking to Claire's untutored eye like a graph from one of the financial papers.

'Any fibrillation or VT?' he asked the ambulanceman.

'None seen, Doctor.'

'Good. Let's get him inside as quickly as possible. Put him into cubicle four, will you?'

He stood aside to let the stretcher be lifted down, then turned to Claire.

'Are you a relative?' he asked, very gently.

'No. He collapsed in front of me.'

'I'd like to speak to you, after I've examined the patient. Can you stay for a little while?'

'Yes.' Her voice was tremulous. 'Yes, I can.'

'Thanks,' he said briefly, and jumped down from the vehicle and followed the stretcher.

One of the nurses showed Claire into a small, bare office, where she began to shake violently. The whole incident had been so shocking, and then to see *him* there!

'Are you all right, my dear?' asked the nurse, her voice concerned. 'You've gone as white as a sheet. Would you like me to bring you a cup of tea?'

Claire nodded blankly, and thanked the nurse automatically as she came back with a cup and saucer, but it lay untouched on the desk as she sat there, hopelessly dazed.

Presently the door opened and he was standing there, looking down at her and smiling.

'You!' he said.

So he wasn't going to pretend that he didn't recognise her, she thought with relief. Instinctively, she felt that this man would always be honest with her.

Under his white coat she could see that he was wearing a checked cotton shirt and olive green cords. Again she was struck by the physical presence of him. He looked so alive, and strong and dependable.

He walked over to her and saw the tea-cup.

'You haven't touched your tea,' he remarked.

Claire shook her head. 'Will he . . . Will Mr Phillips be all right?' she asked, her face chalky white.

'Well, the next twenty-four hours will be crucial, but he's in the best place possible,' he answered noncommittally but kindly. He looked at his wristwatch. 'Look, I can't possibly let you go home in that condition, and I'd like you to tell me what happened. My SHO is putting a drip up on him just now. Let me take you over to the canteen—I need my lunch before this afternoon's ward round, and I might be able to rustle you up a hot cup of tea. By the way, my name's Luke Hayward.'

She looked up and gave him a watery smile. 'Claire Scott,' she said politely. 'Thank you very much, I'd like that.'

She had never been in a hospital canteen before, and was slightly taken aback at the level of noise and activity which greeted her. Luke Hayward led her over to a small, quiet table, well away from the counter, and sat her down.

'I'll just go and find you some tea. Do you want any lunch?'

She shook her head.

While he joined the queue, she looked around at all the crowded tables. There were groups of chattering nurses, in a huge variety of different coloured uniform dresses and belts. Some sat with doctors. Other tables seated young women and men with short white coats, who Claire supposed must be the medical students.

Perhaps it was a naïve impression, she thought, but everyone looked so animated. She was used to spending lunch-breaks on a shoot with other models who sipped at mineral water, and filed their nails and looked bored.

Luke came back with a tray and placed a cup in front of her. For himself he unloaded an enormous plate full of food with masses of vegetables and potatoes, with fruit to follow. Claire's eyes widened slightly. Surely he wasn't going to eat all that! It was more the sort of meal you expected a labourer to eat. The men she usually mixed with picked at a chef's salad and then consumed a bottle of wine!

Luke must have seen her expression, because his eyes twinkled.

'Don't worry,' he told her, 'I haven't usually got quite such a gargantuan appetite, but I was called to coronary care first thing and missed breakfast, and only had a scratch supper last evening. Drink some of your tea now.'

She took a sip. It was the colour of treacle and tasted as though it were composed of treacle too, but she had never enjoyed a cup of tea so much.

Luke ate his meal quickly, like a man used to hurrying, then pushed his plate away and turned the full force of his grey-green eyes on her.

'Feel better?' he asked, and she nodded.

'Do you want to tell me what happened?'

She recited the events of earlier that day as succinctly as possible. 'But I felt so useless,' she told him. 'So impotent, because I wasn't able to help him in any way.'

'And just what did you do, exactly?' he questioned.

'After I'd told that young boy to call for the ambulance, I loosened Mr Phillips' collar, wiped his face and sat there holding his hand until help arrived. That's all,' she finished glumly.

'Claire,' he said, quite seriously, 'if you'd been a State Registered Nurse, you couldn't have done any more for him. You did all the right things, and by instinct. Most important of all, he knew that someone was there, caring for him.'

'Did I? Did I really?' She looked anxiously into his eyes, but she could only see the truth reflected there.

He nodded, and she drank the last mouthful of her tea, and gave him an enormous smile.

'You didn't look very happy at dinner the other evening,' he observed. 'Why was that?'

Claire looked at his strong, firm features, the

broad set of his shoulders and the penetrating eyes. Suddenly she found herself telling him everything. Telling him about feelings which she hadn't even acknowledged to herself. And about those she had—about her general dissatisfaction with her life, and her job as a model. And how most of the people she mixed with cared for nothing more than money, and image.

Luke let her talk and talk. She hadn't spoken to anyone like that for years, not since her father had died. And all the time he listened intently, occasionally nodding.

Eventually she stopped and looked at him, a rueful smile on her lips. 'I'm sorry,' she said, her blue eyes shining brilliantly, 'I didn't mean to place you in the role of father confessor over lunch!'

He ignored the joke and sat there studying her for a minute longer, noting her ice-blue sweater and the glossy abundance of copper curls which fell around her shoulders. Then he leaned over towards her and spoke very softly.

'Claire,' he said, 'forgive me if this sounds like a ludicrous suggestion, but—have you ever thought of becoming a nurse?'

She had not known that he had stood there for almost five minutes on the top step of the main entrance, lost in thought as he watched the tail lights of her taxi disappear into the traffic, wondering what on earth had possessed him to make such a suggestion to her, advising her to come and train at St Anthony's. He had seen her eyes light up eagerly and she had looked up at him like a little lost puppy.

Was it because she too came from a divorced home, a family in splinters? He had found all the commitment and unity a family provided from hospital life. Could it fulfil her in the same way?

Damn and blast, why the hell hadn't he just asked her for a date?

Because she was too young. Because a girl like that was probably sick of being asked for a date by every man she met.

Luke had been a doctor long enough to realise that the fleeting gift of beauty was inconsequential without substance. Beneath the sophisticated veneer he had seen the silent appeal in Claire's lonely eyes. She needed a friend, not a lover. But if she arrived as his protégée, it could make life difficult.

Still, was she really likely to give up modelling—to don a uniform and work all the hours that God sent, as a nurse? If the idea appealed for even half a day, it would be no more than the capricious whim of a very young and impressionable girl, soon to be forgotten when her tall boyfriend reappeared.

The slender young staff nurse from Casualty had appeared at Luke's elbow, her brown eyes seductive beneath the pert blonde fringe.

'Excuse me, Dr Hayward,' she said, smiling, 'but Switchboard says your bleep isn't working, and the lab have some urgent results for you, and must speak to you personally.'

He nodded and re-entered the building, his hands deep in the pockets of his cords, his white coat flapping as he strode down the corridor in search of a phone, his ludicrous suggestion already forgotten.

CHAPTER THREE

SEEING Luke standing there outside the cubicle had made Claire's heart start hammering loudly in her chest, and as she walked briskly alongside Anna Hunter she tried to behave as normally as she could—attempting, without much success, to subdue her rapid breathing.

His physical presence, as always, had sent her into a complete spin. She had known that he was a physician, and she had been assigned to a medical ward, so it was inevitable that their paths would cross sooner or later. She just hadn't been prepared for it to happen on her first day on the wards, or for the sudden rise in her pulse rate.

Luke hadn't spoken to her, but she couldn't miss the fleeting look of amazement which had appeared in his eyes. She was certain that he had expected her to totally dismiss his suggestion that she become a nurse. He had probably forgotten all about her after that day.

And she wouldn't have expected him to say 'hello'. Even in the short time since she had been at St Anthony's, she had realised just how rigidly stratified hospital life was.

They had been taught the rudiments of etiquette in class, and this morning Anna Hunter had reminded her that nurses did not call each other anything but 'Nurse' on the wards. Sister was always formally called just that, and senior doctors certainly did not pass the time of day with the most junior of student nurses in the middle of the consultant's ward round! Claire sighed as she recalled how strong and how gorgeous Luke had appeared, standing next to the note-trolley, the thick golden-brown hair waving on to the collar of his white coat.

As she and Anna pushed open the swing doors into the canteen, Claire wondered if Luke was involved with the pale blonde girl she had seen him with in the restaurant. He might even be married.

The sharp pain which this thought produced made her pray fervently that he wasn't. But he had been with three women that evening, and a good-looking man of his age was bound to be involved with someone.

Fortunately, her schedule for the next two days was frantically busy, and there certainly wouldn't be time to spend mooning over Luke Hayward.

She was looking forward to this weekend off—when she started on the wards full-time next week a weekend off would become like gold-dust—probably only every fourth week. She must make the most of it, and she was looking forward to moving into her new flat. It was slightly smaller than her old one, but it was situated in the middle of an elegant square with a lovingly tended garden in the centre. And the view from her bedroom window was incredible—she could see the foot of the hill and beyond to the mysterious swathes of netting which formed the aviary at the Zoo, and in the distance, London's buildings and skyscrapers, with the Post Office Tower standing tall and proud like a rocket.

She had elicited the help of both Mary Wells and Simon to help her move—the latter claiming that he could drive the more delicate items along himself, to save them being damaged in the furniture van. Claire had thanked him enthusiastically, but wondered just how many trips he would have to do, since his low, narrow sports car was fairly short on baggage space!

By midday, every piece of furniture and clothing which she possessed sat in packing cases in the middle of her new sitting-room, so that the place resembled a jumble sale!

They all three set to work with a will, and by six o'clock some kind of order had been imposed. Simon had bought her an enormous bunch of white lilies, and these she placed in a tall black vase in front of the big windows in the sitting-room.

Claire walked in from the kitchen, wiping her hands on her apron. 'I've found the box with the teapot and cups,' she said, looking around vaguely. 'But I haven't managed to locate any tea to put in them!' She smiled apologetically.

Simon looked at his watch. 'Tell you what,' he said. 'The pubs are open. Why don't I buy you both a drink?'

'I'd love one,' said Mary immediately, dimpling at Simon.

They all queued up to wash the grime from their hands and make their hair look presentable.

'Simon spends more time looking in the mirror than we do!' joked Mary in her down-to-earth way, and Simon grinned sheepishly.

It occurred to Claire that she had never seen him teased quite so relentlessly as Mary had teased him that afternoon, and she noted with some surprise that he actually seemed to enjoy it.

They walked down the road to a large pub on the corner. The last of the shops were shutting up for the night and the restaurants were preparing to open. There was a soft warmth in the air, with the promise of a hot day to follow. They were a companionable threesome, and linked arms until they reached the pub.

Simon went up to fetch the drinks and Claire and Mary found a table beneath a stained glass window, which sent pools of bright clear colour on to the dark polished wood of the table.

'He's gorgeous!' whispered Mary enthusiastically. She looked anxiously at Claire. 'You and he? Are you . . .?'

'No, we're not,' interrupted Claire hurriedly, smiling at Mary's embarrassment. 'We're—to use that awful phrase—just good friends.'

Simon carried three drinks of lager over from the bar and sat down. Claire sipped her drink and sat there quietly, watching as the other two tried to outdo each other with jokes about doctors!

She had never seen Simon so animated. His girlfriends had all been tall, fragile-looking fashion-plates, a complete contrast to Mary, sitting there happily in old jeans and a sweat-shirt. She was a petite girl with a glossy wing of raven hair, big grey eyes and a wide, sunny smile. One of her hobbies, it seemed, was gardening, and Claire listened in astonishment when Simon said that he had an allotment in Shepherd's Bush.

'You never told me that!' exclaimed Claire.

'You never asked me!' he retorted, his eyes on Mary.

He invited them both for supper, but Claire said she was tired.

'I've still got lots of sorting out at the flat to do, and I want to bone up—if you'll excuse the pun—on the digestive system before I start on Belton on Monday.'

The other two didn't look as though they minded her excuse one bit, she observed wryly.

'Claire's the class swot,' said Mary. 'She came top in the end of Block exams.'

Simon turned to her. 'Did you really? That's absolutely marvellous, Claire! I had no idea you were any good at exams.' He sounded genuinely pleased for her.

'Neither did I,' she told them. 'But I find I just love anatomy and physiology. Let's just hope I can apply it to the practical side of nursing.'

She left them outside the pub and walked back up to the flat. Twinkling stars were faintly discernible in the sky. For one impetuous moment she almost felt like taking the longer route home, past the restaurant where she had first seen Luke, wondering if he ate there regularly. Then she scolded herself silently for thinking like a lovestruck little schoolgirl.

Lovestruck. An odd choice of word, she thought as she let herself in through her new front door.

But an accurate one.

On Monday morning she started on Belton full-time, and began to learn a little more about the daily routine of the ward.

Every second of every hour was taken up with something. Each one of the twenty-four patients had to be washed, fed and cared for, and this was the basic job of the nurses. The doctors were there to diagnose and prescribe treatment, and this treatment was then carried out by the nurses.

There might have been time to do everything were it not for a chronic shortage of staff, and the medical emergencies which could arise at any time. Claire quickly discovered that the entire staff for the morning shift could consist of Sister or staff nurse, a third-year and two very inexperienced first-years. Sometimes they were lucky enough to be sent 'help', but this invariably took the form of an auxiliary who didn't know the ward properly and was not allowed to give out drugs or to do dressings.

Claire realised that she would have to learn to walk around the ward at the same breakneck pace as the other nurses, who seemed to be in perpetual motion, as though they were on roller skates.

Sister Thompson always tried to take the student

nurses for half an hour's teaching in the afternoon, when there was an overlap with the late shift. She was a fierce but tremendously kind woman, who expected only the very best from her nurses, and usually got it.

On Wednesday, Sister Thompson was on a late duty and so the report was given by Staff Nurse Lee, a young woman in her mid-twenties, who wore a shiny engagement ring on a chain around her neck, and managed to bring her fiancé into any conversation she could.

'Hello, Nurse Scott,' she said briefly, then bowed her neatly shorn head to look at the work-book. 'I've put you with Nurse Hunter again. I'd like you both to make beds, please, and then help out with general baths. All right?'

'Thank you, Staff,' answered Claire politely, and went off to find Anna Hunter. She located her outside the linen cupboard where she was piling great heaps of newly laundered sheets, pillowcases and bedspreads. They started at the top end of the ward, stripping each bed in turn.

'Haven't seen you since last week. Did you have a good weekend?' asked Anna, as she bundled a dirty sheet into the linen skip.

'Yes, lovely, thank you,' said Claire. 'Did you?'

'Awful! I was on a late on Saturday, followed by an early on Sunday. Old Staff Nurse Droopy-drawers was in a foul mood because she wanted to be with her beloved Nigel, choosing wallpaper. I'm shattered today. Still, I've got a long weekend coming up.' Anna glanced at her fob watch.

'Better get a move on—it's Stellingworth's grand round today.'

Claire's heart skipped a beat when she heard the grand round mentioned. Perhaps she would see Luke. She worked quickly and efficiently, watching the more experienced third-year for any short cuts.

They were halfway down the ward when Claire recognised one of the patients. 'Why, it's Mr Lucas, isn't it?' she asked. What a difference five days could make—she could scarcely believe that it was the same man. He sat in a chair by the side of his bed, still slightly breathless, but needing no oxygen and with a vastly improved colour.

He nodded. 'You're the little nurse who washed me on me first day, ain't you?' he asked.

'Yes, that's right,' smiled Claire. It was the first time that a patient had ever called her Nurse, and it gave her a real feeling of pride.

After they had finished the beds, Anna helped Claire put an elderly patient in the bath. His limbs were rigid and he stared straight ahead, drooling a little from the left side of his mouth.

'Mr Poole has had a bad stroke,' Nurse Hunter explained. 'But the physiotherapist likes us to keep him as mobile as possible. If you give him a quick bath, I'll go and do the four-hourly temperatures and pulses, and be back in time to help you get him out and dressed.'

'Thanks,' said Claire, and squirted some bubble bath into the water. She gently began to wash the old man, pushing the flannel between his contracted fingers. Mrs Haynes had taught them that a patient should always be treated with the utmost respect and dignity, whether he appeared to understand what was going on or not. And so Claire began to chat to him, telling him her name and talking about the weather, and what was happening in the news that day.

Anna came back ten minutes later and helped Claire get him into pyjamas and back into his wheelchair.

'Come and join me in the clinic-room when you've given him a drink. Oh, and don't forget to write how much he takes on his fluid chart!'

Claire nodded and wheeled Mr Poole into the sunny day-room. She bent down to reposition his feet and was just getting up again when she heard footsteps approaching and, as she stood up, she turned and there was Luke behind her, his green-grey eyes scrutinising her.

'You—again!' He smiled at her. 'Young Nurse Scott.'

He looked crumpled and rumpled and very slightly disreputable. His tie was loose and his chin was dark with five o'clock shadow. His eyes looked incredibly weary.

'You look terrible,' she said, without thinking.

His eyes crinkled at the corners at her frankness. No one had spoken to him like that for years, and normally he would never have tolerated a comment like this from such a junior nurse. But this girl was different.

'I've been up all night,' he explained briefly,

and looked her up and down. 'How are you? Are you enjoying it? You look very efficient in your uniform, I must say.'

She blushed. 'Do I? I don't feel very efficient, I can tell you! I've been given a pile of textbooks that seems as high as Mount Everest! I don't think I'm ever going to learn it all.' She looked at him, and her dazzling blue eyes were serious. 'But I love it so far, really love it.'

She did too, Luke thought. She really looked happy—like a different girl. 'It obviously wasn't such a ludicrous suggestion after all, then?' he asked.

Claire shook her head and smiled. 'Only for about an hour! I rang the School of Nursing the next day and had an interview the following week. I managed to convince them I was serious about the idea! They took some convincing. They were able to offer me a cancellation and I had a place within the month, and—here I am!'

'So I see.' He couldn't take his eyes off her. 'I suppose they thought you were crazy, throwing up something like modelling for nursing?'

She nodded. 'Everyone—my parents, my agent, even the Director of Nursing Education—was sceptical for a bit. They automatically assumed that I'd never be able to manage on a nurse's salary.'

'And can you?'

'No,' she joked. 'It's a diabolical pittance!' And they both laughed.

'I'd better go now,' Claire said apologetically,

tugging at her crisp white apron. 'I must give Mr Poole a drink and Nurse Hunter will be waiting for me in the clinic-room.'

'Yes, of course you must. I'll see you soon.' Luke gave her that heart-wrenching grin of his.

She smiled back at him and walked up the ward towards the kitchen.

So she was conscientious too. He hated the nurses who would stand around and chat and bat their eyelashes, while the needs of the patients went unanswered. Perhaps he'd known too many nurses like that in the past.

He stood there for a moment watching her, her straight back, her slim waist, and the long legs in black stockings. She was so beautiful, with a kind of innocent freshness about her.

He thought back to his night in Intensive Care and the girl they had fought all night to save. She couldn't have been very much younger than Claire, but they might have come from different planets.

He remembered how he'd left her. Alive—but only just. A few strands of dyed peroxide hair clinging to her forehead, exhausted and clammy and sweating after the stomach wash-out.

She had swallowed a bottle of pain-killers, in order to 'show' her boyfriend—a weak, spotty youth who had come in reeking of beer, and not seeming to care tuppence for the girl fighting for her life in the cubicle behind him. Luke had felt like punching him in the teeth.

And now all he felt like doing was having a hot bath and getting away from the sickness and brutality of life.

But that, of course, was impossible. He had outpatients' clinics to do and ward rounds to get to, juniors to chase and results to act on. Perhaps he just needed a holiday.

Maybe he should ask the lovely Nurse Scott to go with him, he mused, then remonstrated silently with himself. He had made a conscious choice a long time ago and he wasn't about to start changing the scheme of things at this stage in his life.

He began to walk back up the ward. There would just be time for him to dash over to his room to shave, before he was due in Casualty.

CHAPTER FOUR

FOUR WEEKS just flew by, and it came as a shock to Claire to realise that she had been on Belton for a month and was due another weekend off. She had hardly seen Luke at all in that time, and had wondered vaguely if he might be avoiding her. But why should he?

If he came on the ward the most senior nurse always dealt with him. She was aware of somehow feeling let down. She wondered what she had expected to happen—that he would appear on her doorstep with flowers? If so, she had been disappointed.

She had spoken to him once, briefly, in the canteen. She and Mary had been sitting at morning coffee together, when Claire realised that Luke had been having a solitary drink on the other side of the room. He had to pass their table on his way out and he had stopped to say hello. Claire was furious with herself for blushing madly.

'Still keeping you busy, are they?' Luke had smiled at her.

'They certainly are! Luke, I'd like you to meet Mary Wells. Mary, this is Luke Hayward.'

Mary and Luke had said hello, and then he had left.

'Mm—who's the hunk?' Mary's eyes had been frankly interested.

'Oh, just the Medical Reg on Stellingworth's firm. He—er—recommended a textbook to me once,' Claire had lied.

She had been aware of the curious expression in Mary's eyes, but she had said no more about him. And anyway, what was there to tell? He obviously just wasn't interested.

Anyway, she decided firmly, she certainly wasn't going to waste the whole weekend worrying about what Luke Hayward might or might not be doing. She was looking forward to a lazy time and a lie-in on Sunday with all the papers—heaven!

On Friday at exactly four-thirty, Sister came out of her office and shooed Claire and the other three nurses off the ward.

As she walked down the wide corridor, where solemn oil portraits of former hospital dignitaries adorned the walls, Claire felt a warm and unaccustomed glow of contentment. She felt absolutely exhausted, but this was coupled with a satisfying feeling of achievement. She had completed her first month and she hadn't killed anyone! She was a nurse—and she loved it!

And then she saw him walking towards her. He was right at the other end of the corridor, but she would have recognised that distinctive physique anywhere. His long legs covered the distance between them quickly. He even walked like an athlete, she thought.

As he approached, his eyes creased at the corners

and he gave her a smile, a gloriously intimate smile, as though they shared some incredible secret.

He stopped in front of her and looked at his watch.

'Hello, young Nurse Scott,' he grinned at her. 'Just off home, are you?'

Claire pouted. She wished he wouldn't keep alluding to her age. 'I'll be nineteen in January,' she said pointedly, and watched him as he shook his head from side to side.

'Nineteen,' he murmured. For a moment it appeared as though he were about to carry on walking, when, to her joy and astonishment, he turned to her and said, without preamble, 'Are you doing anything this evening?'

Words she had listened to countless times before became original, precious poetry because Luke Hayward had said them. She shook her head and a wisp of hair tickled the back of her long neck.

'No. No, I'm not. Why?'

Luke regretted the words as soon as he had spoken them, but then, staring down at her face, he found himself wanting to kiss the endearing tilt of her nose.

'Would you like to come out for a drink with me? We could drive west out of London, and find a pub on the river. It'll give you a chance to ask me anything you like about St Anthony's.' He wondered just who he was kidding. 'What do you say?'

'I can't think of anything I'd rather do,' she smiled, unable to be anything other than completely direct with this man, unable and unwilling to waste time and to take part in the subterfuge and intrigue of the dating game.

She gave him her address and he wrote it down and arranged to pick her up at seven.

He strode across the quadrangle to his room, both elated and fuming—furious with himself for wanting to take out a girl who was nearly half his age. He was thirty-three and he was a fool. He had known which duty she would be on, which route she would take. And he had been there, waiting.

But the exasperation melted into excitement, as he thought about where he might take her that evening.

Claire, who had spent two years as a model parading on catwalks and staring into the lens of a camera in front of crowds of onlookers, had never felt so shot with nerves as she hurled one outfit after the other on to the bed. Her hands were shaking and it took a great deal of concentration just to gulp down a cup of coffee.

Eventually she decided on her well worn, much loved jeans, teamed with a filmy white Indian shirt which had filigree silver embroidery at the neck and cuffs. After all, he had suggested a drink in a pub—not dinner at the Ritz!

Then she rushed around the flat, dusting away imaginary bits of fluff, plumping up cushions, and moving a fern five times until it was back in its original position.

At that moment there was a long ring on the

doorbell and, with a last look in the mirror above the fireplace, Claire ran downstairs to greet him.

She opened the door to see Luke standing there, in faded jeans like her own and wearing a scruffy brown leather flying jacket. As always, she was struck by his physical presence and the vitality of his nearness.

The thick golden-brown hair was slightly mussed, and then she noticed the reason why—under his arm he held a white crash helmet and there was a smaller scarlet helmet tied to the back of a huge, gleaming motorbike which was parked by the side of the road.

She gazed at it for a moment and then burst out laughing. 'I don't believe it!' she said. 'Respectable Registrar rides racy motorbike!'

'Don't you like it?' he asked. 'Did you expect me to arrive in a suit, driving a smart car? I've got one of those too,' he added as an afterthought. 'Are you disappointed?'

'Do I look disappointed? And am I dressed for a smart car?' she pointed to her own jeans. 'Where are we going?'

'To Runnymede. It's near Windsor. You'll need a jacket, though. It can get cold on the back.'

She ran upstairs and collected a warm anorak, then hurried back down to him, her heart thumping with excitement.

Luke watched her as she crammed the scarlet helmet on to her curls with careless abandon. He hadn't told her that he had only bought the helmet that very afternoon, after he left her. The bike, lovingly polished and maintained since his student days, was his transport for solitary journeys —instant escapism down fast motorways. It was the sleek sports car which was usually reserved for dates.

'I nearly brought the car, but changed my mind at the last minute,' he shouted as he revved the machine up.

'I'm glad you did,' murmured Claire as she climbed up behind him and clasped her arms tightly around his waist as they roared away. It was blissful to be able to rest her cheek against the rough leather of his jacket, and to watch London speeding by. Past Regent's Park and Lords cricket ground, and out on to the Marylebone Road, where Luke opened up the throttle and the cold air rushing into her lungs made her gasp.

They crossed the river at Hammersmith, and rode on out west, all the time in glorious sunshine with the landscape becoming flatter and the skies more vast as they neared Heathrow Airport.

They turned off at a roundabout, and suddenly they were in the relative peace of Runnymede, the road fringed with the narrow silver Thames on one side and by green fields and gentle slopes on the other. Claire had visited it once before, years ago, after seeing her father off at the airport. The signing of the Magna Carta had been something she remembered vaguely from school, and the spot where this had taken place had meant little to her. But she had been moved to tears by the simple stone memorial to the late President Kennedy, even though he had been assassinated long before she was born.

Luke stopped in the car park of a pub which was right on the river itself and turned to see her pulling off the helmet. He'd not wanted the ride to end. It had been marvellous—feeling the powerful strength of the machine and the warmth of her arms around him so tightly.

'OK?' he asked, and she nodded, her pink cheeks glowing.

The saloon bar was surprisingly uncrowded, but it was still fairly early, and they chose a table on a balcony upstairs, overlooking the river.

Luke fetched their drinks and they clinked glasses and said 'cheers', then sipped them, and sat for a few moments in silence, taking in the lapping water and the changing quality of the light as dusk hovered closer and closer.

'I love your motorbike,' Claire told him as she swirled the ice around in her glass. 'She looks very special. Have you had her a long time?'

He looked delighted. 'How very perspicacious of you, Miss Scott! Not only have you used the correct gender, but you've described her very accurately. She *is* very special—a Kawasake Z 900. I bought her with some money from my grandmother when I was twenty-one, instead of putting the money down as a deposit for a flat. That was the beginning of a relationship which has lasted for twelve years.' He took a sip of his beer and leaned back lazily in his chair.

Claire did some hasty arithmetic. That meant he

was thirty-three! No wonder he kept making so many comments about her age. She would have to show him that she could be as mature as any twenty-five-year-old.

'What happened to Mr Phillips?' she asked. It had been bothering her for some time.

Luke looked momentarily puzzled. 'Mr Phillips? Oh, you mean your gentleman with the heart attack.'

'Myocardial infarction,' she corrected him, and she saw his lips twitch.

'Yes, of course—thank you. I keep forgetting that you're a nurse now,' he replied gravely, and took another sip of beer. 'Well, he stayed in coronary care under observation for a couple of weeks, and then we sent him home. I'm seeing him in Outpatients next week, so I'll be able to tell you more then.' He found himself sitting forward, just so that he could catch that elusive waft of her scent.

'Are you hungry?' he asked. 'Why don't we have something to eat here? There's a very good restaurant.'

'We aren't really dressed for it, are we?' Claire imagined they would stick out like two sore thumbs if they went in to dinner wearing jeans and with windswept hair.

Luke waved a hand dismissively through the air, in an unexpectedly Gallic gesture. 'Don't worry about that. I've been eating here since I was a student. I used to hoard bits of my grant to eat here on high days and holidays. And Claude, who's now the owner, is an old friend.' His smile was irresistible.

'All right, then. But let me go and try to tame my curls first,' she smiled.

In the powder-room she pulled a comb through the tangled ringlets and looked at the unaccustomed flush of excitement which tinged her pale cheeks. She found herself wondering jealously who he had saved up to bring here, on high days and holidays, as he had put it.

He led her into the dining-room and they were given a window seat with an uninterrupted view of the Thames, whose glimmering had begun to fade as night softly fell.

They ordered simply—first asparagus in a meltingly rich hollandaise sauce, followed by poached salmon, new potatoes and mange-touts. Luke poured iced Chablis, and as they drank and broke pieces of brown bread with their fingers, they talked, unable to keep their eyes off each other.

He asked her about her mother's reaction to her entering the nursing profession.

Claire was touched and slightly surprised that he recalled everything that she had blurted out to him that day in the canteen. She laughed as she told him what her mother had said.

'She asked me, in an astounded tone, how I could possibly face all those injections and bedpans and blood. I told her not to be silly, that she was talking about a tiny, tiny part of it.'

He looked at her. She had all the exuberance and

impetuosity of youth. 'You haven't been disappointed, then?' he asked her softly.

Grey-green eyes met blue ones. 'Not a bit,' she replied, equally softly.

Their plates of raspberry sorbet lay neglected. She began to ask him about his family.

He shook his head a little. He felt as though she had lulled him into some hypnotic trance. He stood up abruptly.

'Claire, will you excuse me for just a moment? I must go and leave a message for Claude. Order some coffee for us—and a liqueur for yourself, if you like.'

She gave him a tiny smile and, feeling slightly confused, watched him go. She noticed at least two other women pause, their eyes rapacious as they took in his muscular frame, his confident stride.

Luke walked quickly outside, back on to the balcony. All the tables were now full with chattering groups. He inhaled deeply. He needed time to think. It had been a mistake to bring her here tonight.

He leaned over the balcony. Some revellers were tying a boat up. He heard a girl's shrill giggling as she tottered on to dry land. He stood for a few moments in silence, then reluctantly walked back inside towards the restaurant, via reception, where the sight of him caused the young girl on the desk to break into an excited babble.

'Why, Monsieur le Docteur! We are not expecting you. Why did you not tell us? Monsieur Claude, he is not here.'

He felt relieved. At least he wouldn't have to face Claude's inquisitive eyes. In fluent and accentless French, he told her that his visit had been spontaneous, and that he would telephone Claude.

He made his way back to the restaurant and stood in the doorway for a moment, watching her. She hadn't seen him, and as she sat in the window, he was reminded vividly of a painting he had seen a long time ago, as a boy.

It had been just after the divorce. His aunt had taken him to London for lunch—a schoolboy's lunch of cake and ice-cream. Afterwards they had visited an art gallery. Luke had been ignorant of art, and she had wondered if he might be overwhelmed by the paintings. But he had not been overwhelmed. Instead he had fallen in love with the *Beata Beatrice*.

He stood watching as Claire gazed at the river, her chin resting in her hand. Her lips were dreamy and the creamy skin provided a strong contrast to the red hair. The dark pink light of the setting sun lit her from behind, turning the ends of her hair into fire, and giving her a peculiarly spiritual quality. She *was* Rossetti's Beatrice.

He knew then that he wanted her. He wanted to kiss her, to make love to her—to run his fingers through those glorious curls. He wanted to possess her completely, and it was pointless. He was leaving St Anthony's in six short weeks, to begin a new life.

He must not see her again.

With a tight knot in the pit of his stomach, he began to walk back towards their table.

Claire lay in bed, watching the curtains as they billowed gently in the breeze. What had happened to make Luke change so suddenly?

Nothing had actually been said, but she felt as though she had spent the evening with two different men.

One moment he had been describing his days as a medical student, and teasing her and making her laugh. She had always dreamed of finding a man who was so easy to be with. She had felt as though she were poised on the brink of some magical discovery.

And then he had got up so quickly and had left the room, and when he came back he had changed. Oh, he was polite and courteous, even amusing. But it was as though he had retreated behind a wall of glass—he had become untouchable.

What had she done? What could she have said? The only incident remotely resembling any discord had been when she had asked him about his parents.

'They're divorced,' he had said shortly—and had changed the subject.

When he came back to their table he had smiled at her gently and had dropped his bombshell.

'I shall remember this evening when I'm in bonny Scotland.'

Claire had flicked the crumbs out of her napkin and smiled—the moment drawn indelibly on her mind.

'Oh, that's nice,' she had remarked. 'For a holiday?'

'No, Claire. For years.'

For years. For years. For years. The words echoed around in her head and wouldn't leave her alone, like some irritating pop song.

Luke had gone on to tell her that he was going to take up a post as Senior Registrar on a Professorial Unit in Glasgow. With hope in her heart, she prayed that it wouldn't preclude a relationship between them. But she seemed to detect a chilling finality in the way he spoke.

The ride home had been cold. This time she had derived no warmth from his body, and her teeth were chattering violently by the time they drew up outside her flat.

'You're freezing,' he said softly. 'Better go in and have some cocoa, or something.'

'Won't you come in for a nightcap?' she suggested brightly, hoping that her voice wasn't betraying the fear that she felt. That he wouldn't ask to see her again.

He shook his head and took the crash helmet from her. 'I've an early ward round to do tomorrow—I'd better go. Thanks very much for coming.' He grinned that devastating grin of his and was gone, the roar of the engine drowning her tiny disappointed words of thanks.

She turned her pillow over and buried her face in it, wondering if he thought her some sort of fool. Had he just felt obliged to take her out, because he felt responsible for her?

She hadn't bothered to hide her feelings for him. Perhaps he was worried that she might become an embarrassment to him—a young girl following him around.

Well, he needn't worry. She certainly wasn't going to make a nuisance of herself. And there were only six weeks to go before he went off to Glasgow.

She wondered how long the aching in her heart would last.

CHAPTER FIVE

CLAIRE STILL had the whole weekend free and she decided to decorate the sitting-room. She must try and be rational about things. She had a strong crush on a man and it had not been reciprocated. Rejection—it happened all the time, and to some of the nicest people!

She had obviously misread the signs, she decided with a sigh as she opened a tin of paint.

She painted all day Saturday, listening to the radio and enjoying the mindless rhythm of the brush slapping emulsion on to the walls. She had chosen a soft yellow. Her curtains and sofas were a bright peacock blue of slub silk and the sunny walls provided an unexpected but magnificent contrast. She made a mental note to buy peacock feathers to stand in the fireplace.

By evening, however, her euphoria seemed to have evaporated and when she had tidied away the pots and brushes, she could do no more than pick half-heartedly at a pizza.

She washed up, then sat down at the kitchen table to write a letter to her mother. The smell of paint was still very powerful, even though she had opened all the windows, and her head began to throb. She didn't find it easy to communicate with her mother at the best of times, but tonight the task seemed impossible. She could think of nothing but Luke. Everywhere she looked she could picture his face, his lips, and his enigmatic eyes.

On Sunday morning she moved the furniture back and spent a couple of hours looking in her textbooks at the respiratory system. From the window she could see a pale, clear sun with clouds scudding furiously past.

The temptation was too much, and pushing her books aside, Claire unlocked her bike and cycled at a snail's pace to the Heath—it was uphill all the way, but the exercise left her glowing.

She parked her bike and took a well-worn route up to the White Pond, where she sat for a while just watching the water, reminded of the lights sparkling on the Thames, and of Luke.

As she strolled back, taking great gulps of the summer-scented air, she reflected that the whole world seemed to be divided into couples or dog-owners. On her way to find her bike, she passed one of the big pubs—the tables outside were full of groups of young people, all drinking lager and chewing French bread and laughing.

She wondered what she was doing spending such a beautiful Sunday all on her own. And what of Luke? Was he also on his own? Or had another girl succumbed to his charm? Perhaps even now he was roaring up some country lane, with someone else clinging to him as tightly as she had.

She was relieved when Monday morning arrived. She was on an early duty with Sister Thompson in charge.

Sister gave the nurses a very brief report. 'Staff Nurse Lee is off sick with the 'flu and I'm afraid that means we're two short. I'm trying to get hold of the Nursing Officer, to explain the situation.

'Meanwhile, Mr Bryant has gone home and so has Mr Lucas. We've one empty bed and Mr O'Rourke has been moved down to bed five to make way for the new admission.' She paused for a moment and read from the Kardex in front of her.

'Our new admission is a Mr David Lewis, aged twenty-five. He was admitted during the night, having had one episode of haematemesis—that's vomiting blood, Nurse Scott,' she added, noticing Claire's frown. 'We're just observing him for the time being. He has an intravenous infusion in situ and is on total bedrest until the medics have decided what the cause of the bleeding is.

'Now,' she looked around the room, 'Nurse Hunter and Nurse Scott to make beds and give out the bowls, please. I'd like you to check Mr Churchill's blood pressure, please, Nurse Goldsmith, and assist with bowls, then take Nurse Hunter with you to do the drugs while Nurse Scott gives Mr Lewis a bed-bath.' She paused for breath. 'Thank you all very much.' She smiled at them briefly and they all scurried out.

As Claire sped swiftly up and down the ward, handing out plastic bowls full of warm water to patients, along with silvery kidney dishes containing pink fizzy mouthwash, she realised why most nurses were reed-slim, even though they seemed to eat so much.

There was never a single moment in which to pause. At least three things always needed doing, all at the same time. And as each morning progressed, more and more people added to the busy atmosphere as physiotherapists, porters, doctors and social workers all arrived and were directed to patients by Sister or whoever was in charge.

After the beds were all made and the dirty linen bundled into a skip in the sluice, Claire walked over to the first bed, to where Mr Lewis lay.

She was shocked to see how young he looked. True, Sister had given his age as twenty-five in the report, but she was unprepared for the reality of seeing someone almost the same age as herself, lying pale and sick and helpless in a hospital bed, looped up to a drip and with a vomit bowl lying on the pillow beside him.

He gave her a weak smile. 'Hello,' he muttered. 'Have I died and gone to heaven, or what?'

'Shh!' reprimanded Claire softly. 'You're here to rest and get better. I'm Nurse Scott, and I'm going to give you a wash and shave. All right?'

He nodded and then his eyes fluttered to a close, almost as though the effort of agreeing had exhausted him. As Claire placed the bowl and the mouthwash on top of his locker, she thought how miserably thin and racked his body looked.

She turned her back for a moment, about to pull the curtains round, when she heard a kind of gurgling gasp. 'Nurse,' he said hoarsely, and began to cough, great racking coughs. 'Nurse!'

And then to her horror, bright scarlet blood had begun to spill from his mouth on to the bed, splashing on to her apron and on to the floor, and seeming to fill the whole cubicle with a fearful red haze.

For a split second the moment became frozen and a kind of numb terror took hold of her, then it had passed for ever, and she began to act as she had been taught.

She pulled the emergency buzzer by the side of the bed and quickly drew the curtains round the bed. She knew that the rest of the ward must never be witnesses to the drama and chaos of a medical emergency.

She looked down at David Lewis's face. It was white and clammy. She knew that he was slipping into shock. She put her fingers on his pulse and looked at her watch. A hundred and forty, and weak and fluttery.

And meanwhile the emergency buzzer was sounding insistently and urgently every ten seconds and a red light was flashing above the bed.

Claire thought frantically about what to do next. She remembered that the cause of the cold, white, clammy skin was peripheral shutdown. She wished someone would come.

Shock. The physical manifestations of shock were high pulse and low blood pressure—of course! She carefully pulled out the pillows from behind the patient's head and let the back-rest down. Then she laid him flat and began to wind up the foot of the bed.

He looked dreadful and his breath was coming in faint rasps. Where was everybody? The chatter of the patients had stilled to a hush and the sound of the alarm seemed unnaturally loud.

Just then, in answer to her prayers, Claire heard the sound of running footsteps, and there, pulling back the curtains and breathing deeply, stood Luke. She had never been so glad to see someone in her life.

He took in the great splashes of blood, dramatic against the snowy white bed-linen. He strode over to the man and put his long fingers on the carotid artery in his neck, and began to speed up the intravenous infusion. What had before been the regular drip of normal saline now became a steady stream as it rushed through the tubing into the patient's vein.

'When did this happen? Were you here?' he asked briefly, and Claire nodded. 'Are you the only one around?'

'I think so,' she answered desperately, feeling out of her depth and inadequate. 'What do you want me to do?'

He spoke as he took his stethoscope from his pocket. 'I need to put up a central venous pressure line,' he explained carefully. 'I'd like you to bring me the special CVP pack, together with two green cannulas, cleaning solution and a pair of size nine gloves. Oh, and another litre of normal saline. Have you got all that?'

'Yes, I think so.' Taking deep breaths to calm

herself, Claire hurried into the clinic-room and set about finding what he had asked for. To her relief, everything was so neatly labelled that she found everything, even the CVP pack, which was right at the top of a cupboard.

She arrived back at the cubicle at exactly the same time as a flustered Nurse Goldsmith and an out-of-breath Bill Dixon.

'Dr Hayward!' gasped the third-year nurse. 'Mr Banks has fallen down in the bathroom and given himself a nasty crack on the head. He's unconscious and it looks as though he needs stitches. Nurse Hunter's with him now.'

Luke nodded and walked out to the sink next to the cubicle, where he began washing his hands.

'I see. Go and check him over, will you, Bill?' he said to his houseman, and the young physician sped off down the ward towards the bathrooms. 'Can you ring Intensive Care and try and organise a bed for me, Nurse? I'm going to put in a CVP line here and Nurse Scott can help me. Oh, and for God's sake, can you get on to the Nursing Office and find some more staff from somewhere—this situation is ridiculous!'

Nurse Goldsmith looked rather nervous and went off into the office.

'Right then, Claire,' said Luke in a low, patient voice. 'I just want you to do everything I tell you.'

He talked her through the whole procedure, instructing her to open the sterile gloves and pack, and to pour in the cleaning solution. She gently turned the patient's head to the side, to position him so that Luke could insert the line more easily. She handed him the cannula and watched as he passed it into the vein in the neck.

He worked swiftly and with tremendous precision, it seemed to Claire. All the time he talked to the patient about what he was about to do next, even though Mr Lewis lay in a coma on the narrow hospital bed.

Eventually the line was inserted and pronounced stable. Luke sent Claire off for some tape to secure it, and when she brought it back he was running in normal saline on both lines.

'I need to try and replace some of the fluid volume he's lost through vomiting all that blood,' he explained.

Claire heard the familiar tap-tapping of Sister's footsteps, and puffing furiously, Sister drew back the curtains and surveyed the scene in front of her.

'Good grief!' she exclaimed. 'What a massive haematamasis—will he do?'

Luke nodded. 'I think so. We're trying to get him into Intensive Care now, but I know they were full this morning. You may have to get someone to special him until we can transfer him.'

Sister frowned. 'I was called away to check some urgent morphia on Denning Ward.' She turned to Claire. 'I'll take over here now, Nurse Scott. I'd appreciate it if you could carry on with the routine work. The other patients still need drinks, bedpans and dressings. But you'd better nip off and change your uniform first—you're covered in blood.'

'Yes, Sister.'

As Claire left she could hear Luke telling Sister that the houseman was with a head injury in the bathroom and Sister's response.

'Crikey! It never rains but it pours! That does it—we must have some relief.'

Claire walked quickly along the small back corridor leading off the main corridor and into the nurses' changing-rooms. She unlocked her locker and pulled out a clean dress, apron and collar. As she did so, she caught sight of herself in the mottled old mirror on the wall. She looked as though she had been assisting on the front line of battle and her hair looked as though someone had dragged her through a hedge.

She changed into the clean uniform, washed her face and hands and combed her hair and tied it up tightly. She pinned her cap back on, put her soiled dress into a plastic bag in the locker and set off back to the ward.

As she walked in through the swing doors, she bumped into Luke, who was grinning happily and whistling softly under his breath.

'Are you all right?' he asked, his voice sounding concerned.

Meeting his eyes, she answered, 'Yes.'

'That was a pretty shocking thing to happen to you on your first ward. I thought you acted brilliantly.'

'Thank you.'

'And what's more, I told Sister so.' He looked at her closely. 'Are you sure you're all right?'

'I'm fine.' Claire could hardly tell him that she

could cope with medical crises, especially if she did all the right things. What she couldn't cope with was seeing him every day and wanting him so much. 'What will happen to Mr Lewis?'

'He'll go to Intensive Care, where we'll stabilise him until he's fit enough to undergo a general anaesthetic and surgery. He'll need an operation if, as I suspect, he has a duodenal ulcer. But I'll need to endoscope him first, to confirm the diagnosis.'

Blue eyes met his knowing grey-green ones and she felt a sharp pang. 'I must get back now. The ward's frantic.'

Luke's firm lips curved into a smile. She wondered if he had any idea of the effect his smile had on her. She doubted it.

''Bye,' he said.

Claire knocked on Sister's door, to check what exactly she wanted her to do next.

'Come in!' a voice called.

Sister was seated at her desk and a tall slim nurse stood beside her, her neat ash-blonde head bent over the work book. As she looked up, her lazy grey eyes gave Claire an interested stare and it was as much as Claire could do not to exclaim aloud.

She knew that girl's face and she was pretty sure that the recognition had been mutual.

She would have remembered that slim, athletic build, the small neat ankles and wrist. Remembered the enviable self-possession and the frank gaze she had given Claire on the only other time they had seen each other. And on that occasion they hadn't even been introduced.

Sister looked up, and smiled. 'Nurse Scott,' she said, 'I'd like you to meet Staff Nurse Jilly French. She'll be working here for the time being.'

Their eyes met. It was the girl Claire had seen in the restaurant, with Luke.

CHAPTER SIX

CLAIRE had not been prepared to like the enigmatic Jilly French, but to her surprise she couldn't help warming to the girl. She was the embodiment of everyone's idea of a popular head girl at school.

She was funny, extremely hard-working and scrupulously fair. She didn't ever shirk the practical, less glamorous side of nursing. She would never delegate to a junior nurse a task which she could not face doing herself. Yet her teaching of related anatomy and physiology was second to none. She was friendly, but kept a proper professional distance.

The perfect nurse, thought Claire gloomily. How very appropriate that she should share the company of the perfect doctor!

But while she might find it difficult to dislike Jilly, it didn't stop her feeling jealous of her. For now, of course, as staff nurse, often in charge of the ward, Jilly was the one who accompanied Luke on his ward rounds, Jilly who provided him with coffee and biscuits in the office.

They made a handsome couple—her pale, understated beauty complementing his tall, tanned body. Claire couldn't help noticing how those slanting eyes of Luke's would light up with pleasure whenever Jilly was on duty.

They seemed to have an easy rapport, and once Claire overheard her joking, saying, 'Yes, coach!' and she had hurried away, feeling physically sick.

But despite her troubled heart, she had begun to adapt comfortably to the ward routine. She learnt about the different routines on morning and late duties. She began to know all the patients by name, and what was wrong with them and what treatment they were receiving for their condition, and why.

She soon recognised members of the professional team. She watched the physiotherapists as they gently began to mobilise patients after a serious illness. The process would be aided by the social worker who, as often as not, would sort out such a pressing problem as finding temporary accommodation for a much-loved cat while its owner was away in hospital. Sister explained that if a patient was worrying about little things, then they wouldn't be using their energy properly—on getting better quickly.

One day she was able to go down to the occupational therapy department to observe how the therapist showed patients how to adapt to a disability, yet manage to maintain their independence in the home.

Claire began to get used to the sheer hard physical nature of the job. She might have felt miserable about Luke in quiet moments, but she certainly never had any problems sleeping at night.

She became quite friendly with Bill Dixon. He

was only about five years older than her and this was his first job after qualifying. He was an open-faced, good-humoured Yorkshireman with very curly brown hair and big blue eyes, a bit like a baby. In fact, he told Claire that his three older sisters disrespectfully called him 'Babyface'!

She had had lunch with him in the canteen a couple of times and he had asked her out, but she had refused, foolishly thinking that she wouldn't date anyone else until Luke had gone to Scotland, just in case he asked her.

She had often wondered why she had never seen him in the canteen, until one day when she discovered the answer. Mary had been reading a very good textbook called *Surgical Ward Routine Made Simple* and had discovered that there was a sister book about medical wards and that there was a copy in the hospital library.

Claire had joined the library when she was in the Introductory Block, but hadn't bothered to take any books out. She had always liked owning her books, but, as Mary pointed out, medicine was constantly changing and if she were not careful, she would end up with a very expensive and obsolete collection of textbooks.

She was late going to lunch. A patient had died unexpectedly and she had helped to lay him out. She had left the ward feeling sad, but with a sense of appreciation of her youth and energy and a determination never to take the beauty of life for granted.

She found that she couldn't face the thought of

eating in the hot, crowded canteen on such a brilliantly sunny July day. When the weather was really warm, then the smells of mass catering, the boiled cabbage and sweet puddings with custard, were often unbearably cloying.

Claire bought a salmon and cucumber sandwich from the kiosk in the main hall and a small carton of fresh orange juice. She would just have enough time to go and borrow her book and then take it with her lunch into the small, cloistered garden behind the hospital chapel.

She ran up the steps to the library two by two, her long slim legs bounding athletically. One wall of the library was given over almost entirely to windows, and consequently the enormous room was filled with light and with a distant view over the northern part of the city, with the soft greens of the Heath in the foreground predominating.

She stood quietly behind two medical students in the queue, looking idly round the room, and then her heart gave a leap and began to pound painfully. Her face and hands suddenly felt icy cold and she had to try hard to stop herself from shivering.

For there, sitting at a table in the far corner of the room, sat Luke, his broad shoulders instantly recognisable beneath the anonymous white coat. As always, his golden-brown hair gleamed. It was slightly too long, and she could just discern a few strands on his shirt collar.

He was leaning forward and the whole set of his body was animated. And he had a companion with him. If Claire had needed proof of the relationship she had only to look. It was Jilly French.

She could see that he was using his hands expressively in that distinctive way of his. She remembered how she had been struck by it that night when he had taken her out for supper.

Jilly was sitting forward, leaning on her elbows, that laconic half-smile on her face.

They hadn't seen Claire. She quickly turned and left the library without a backward glance, and somehow made her way to the garden. She sat down on the seat and buried her face in her hands, the orange juice forgotten, the sandwich discarded.

Why, oh, why was she such a stupid little fool? She had been wondering desperately, like a woman obsessed, why Luke had not wanted to repeat their date, and now she had the answer. He had someone else. Someone who had been with him the first time she had ever set eyes on him. A lovely, charming qualified nurse who had probably been going out with him for years.

And why had she, Claire, placed so much importance on what was simply a drink and a meal? One casual date. She might have felt all kinds of attraction towards him, but she had obviously just been imagining that he felt the same way about her. Just wishful thinking really.

He hadn't even tried to kiss her at the end of the evening. And he was memorable just for that, she thought ruefully. The only man who had never tried. And the only man she had prayed would try.

And the reason for all this was now patently

clear. He was involved with someone else. He was the type of man who was loyal and good and true. He was already spoken for, and she had better get that into her thick skull.

Soon he would be gone, and she need never see him again. She was young and she would get over him. And next time Bill Dixon asked her to go out with him, then she would jolly well go.

She looked at her watch. Time to go back. Time to start behaving like an adult, instead of an immature adolescent. She disappeared through the gate in an ancient wall, covered with fragrant honeysuckle.

A starling flew down to where she had sat on the wooden bench, and, cautiously at first, but growing bolder all the time, began to peck through the cellophane to her sandwich.

Luke had seen her, of course. He had felt her presence even before he had noticed her imposing silhouette, the bright hair curling softly. He seemed to have almost an extra sense where she was concerned. But it wasn't just strong magnetism. She made him feel as randy as hell.

He had guessed what she must be thinking, particularly as she hadn't even stopped to renew or take out a book.

Well, let her think what she liked, it was probably easier for them both if she did.

He had deliberately been avoiding long stays on her ward, often choosing very early mornings to look at his patients, before she had started work.

He had three weeks to go. It was pointless to start something now.

If only the sight of her wasn't such an assault on his senses!

With an effort he dragged his mind back to the present and continued talking to Jilly.

CHAPTER SEVEN

CLAIRE went back to work that afternoon, determined once and for all to put Luke Hayward out of her mind. As always, the pace was frantic.

After she had emptied all the catheter bags and charted the urine, she accompanied Sister on the drug round.

'There must always be two nurses to check drugs,' Sister told Claire, her kindly face serious. 'Never cut corners, not even when on night duty and you're *really* overworked. A mistake, once made, can never be rectified. At best you could be in serious trouble as a nurse, possibly with your career in tatters. At worst you could seriously injure or even kill the patient.'

Claire nodded as the older woman continued.

'If you're tired, or have a headache, or your mind is on something else and you've no one checking medication with you—well, the mind boggles at the possible outcome. I once stopped a nurse from diluting an injection of penicillin with potassium instead of plain water. The patient would have died if I hadn't.

'Anyway,' she went on, her familiar smile transforming her plump face, 'now that I've scared the apron off you, I'll put your mind at ease by telling you that as long as you're thorough, and that you double check, you'll be all right. And lastly—' she paused to give emphasis to her next words, 'the golden rule in nursing is—if in doubt then *ask*. Never be afraid to ask—no matter how fierce the Sister is!' She chuckled at this and they began to push the drug trolley up the ward.

Sister showed Claire how to tip the tablets into the lid of the bottle before transferring them to a small plastic medicine pot.

'Never tip them into your hand—your hand could be dirty or sweaty. We have enough problems keeping germs and cross-infection down on the ward—that's why we have to have rules about everything. Do you understand that?'

Claire nodded. 'Yes, Sister.'

They stopped at the end of each patient's bed and consulted the drug chart. At one point Sister placed one of the charts at the bottom of the trolley, saying, 'I must show that to Dr Hayward—he mentioned changing the night sedation earlier.' Quietly, almost as an afterthought, she murmured, 'I must say, I just don't know how I'll get used to someone else after Luke. He's the best Medical Registrar I've had for years. And so kind to the patients too.'

Claire said nothing. It didn't really help to have his praises sung by Sister Thompson! They reached Mr Taylor's bed. Claire took his antibiotics over to him and poured out a glass of water.

'Wotcher, Nurse!' He gave her a wide smile as he took his tablets. 'Heard the good news?'

'What's that, Mr Taylor?' asked Claire, chuckling slightly. His constant good humour always managed to cheer her up.

'I'm off home tomorrow, ain't I, Sister?'

'Yes, you are—and good riddance to you,' joked Sister. 'You've been keeping half the ward awake at night with your jokes. You're to stop smoking and not come back, do you hear me?'

The elderly man's face looked almost bashful. 'I've promised the wife I'll never touch the old weed again. That Dr 'Ayward made me. Proper fierce, 'e was!'

'I'm pleased to hear it,' said Sister grudgingly, and to Claire, 'I just don't know how that man does it, I really don't.'

If she heard one more compliment about the man, she'd scream! thought Claire helplessly.

They walked back to the clinic-room. There was only one injection to give, and Sister watched as Claire drew them up. She had seen how the other nurses snapped the top off the glass phial through their aprons, to avoid scratching their fingers. She pumped the syringe up and down a couple of times before withdrawing the solution, in order to rid it of any air bubbles.

'Would you like to give it?' asked Sister, her eyes twinkling as she saw Claire's mouth open in horror.

Claire gulped and nodded.

It was Mr Armstrong's Vitamin B^{12} injection, explained Sister. He suffered from pernicious anaemia, which meant that he was unable to absorb this vital component through the wall of his stomach. The simple monthly injection prevented him from getting anaemic.

Sister followed Claire behind the cubicle, where she told Mr Armstrong what she was about to do. He turned on to his stomach and Claire exposed the upper part of his buttock. She drew a cross in the air and pointed tentatively to a spot well within the gluteus maximus, then looked up at Sister, who nodded silently and gave her a huge encouraging wink.

She remembered Mr Haynes's words: 'Be positive. Be confident.' She fired the syringe firmly into the upper outer quadrant, withdrew slightly to check that she had not hit a blood vessel, then slowly pushed the solution in. The procedure was finished by a quick rub with some antiseptic solution and then she was helping Sister sit the patient up.

'Thank you, Nurse,' he said.

Claire nodded, unable to hide a smile of delight as she drew back the curtains.

'Oh, and Nurse?'

Claire turned. 'Yes, Mr Armstrong?'

'That's not bad for a first one!' He grinned, and Sister burst into peals of laughter.

'How do you think he knew?' asked Claire, as they made their way back to the clinic-room, their shoulders shaking.

'Nurse Scott—while it might be a bit of an exaggeration to say that Mr Armstrong has had more injections than *I've* had hot dinners, I should think he's fairly experienced! Don't worry, you were fine. At least he didn't jump ten feet into the air!'

Pleased, Claire hurried off to the kitchen, to help Anna Hunter give out the afternoon teas, as the ward domestic was at a Union meeting. Anna was emptying a packet of digestive biscuits on to a plate, and brushing a few crumbs from the side of her mouth.

'You look very chuffed,' she remarked as she filled the teapot with boiling water from the urn.

'I've just given my first injection!' said Claire, executing a small dance on the spot.

'Is that all? I thought you'd won the hospital gold medal, at least. You first-years! Now pass me the sugar and that pile of saucers, and get a move on!'

'Cynic!' retorted Claire, sticking her tongue out.

After tea, she laboriously filled in every single fluid chart and then watched Anna remove an intravenous infusion.

As she washed her hands outside the office, she heard the sound of pounding feet in the corridor and looked up to see three doctors pelting past the doors.

Sister rushed out of her office almost as fast. 'Hunter!' she called, and Anna came running. 'There's a crash call next door on Bradley Ward—go and see if they need an extra pair of hands.

'Nurse Scott, you can go and help Dr Dixon take blood from old Mr Tippett. He's bound to try and punch the doctor—he always does!'

On cue, Bill Dixon appeared carrying a kidney dish full of needles, a 10ml syringe, a tourniquet and various blood bottles and lab forms.

'Hi there, beautiful,' he said softly. 'Are you coming to hold my hand?'

Claire frowned at him and began to lead the way down the ward. 'Don't let Sister hear you chatting up the nurses, or your life won't be worth living!'

He shrugged. 'I'm forced to resort to innuendo—how else am I going to get you to go out with me?' He quickened his pace to draw level with her.

'Try asking me,' she said softly.

He was standing there, looking like a Cheshire Cat who had just won the Pools. 'What time do you finish?' he hissed.

'Four-thirty,' she whispered, and then ducked, as Mr Tippett aimed a hairbrush at Bill's lapel.

Claire tried to be enthusiastic and to look as good as possible for her date with Bill. She wore a beautifully cut black shirtwaister, with sheer black stockings and black patent shoes.

She remembered the bubbling excitement and virtual panic she had felt as she'd changed one outfit for another while waiting for Luke.

But it was most definitely not going to be a successful evening if she was going to think of Luke at every stage. Yesterday Bill had asked her out and she had said she would love to go out with him. So be it. She *would* enjoy herself.

The exam results of the final-year medical students were due out that day, and according to Bill, there was to be 'fun, frolics and high jinks' in the students' bar. 'And lots of champagne,' he had added.

'You are lucky, Claire,' said Mary when she told her. They often had a quick coffee in the canteen after an early duty, before going their separate ways. 'It's tremendously popular, apparently, and by invitation only. Fancy getting an invite in your first year!'

Claire took a sip of black coffee. 'You're not going, I take it?'

Mary gave a smile and looked down at her lap, suddenly shy. 'I'm seeing Simon,' she murmured.

Claire arched her eyebrows. 'I see,' she said meaningfully, and watched her friend's cheeks go scarlet.

Bill called for her punctually. He walked round the sitting-room of her flat, looking closely at her books and her Persian rug.

'Nice place you've got here,' he commented. 'Not all bought on a first-year nurse's pay, I gather?'

'I may tell you my life story later—*if* you're lucky!' she retorted. 'Do you want a drink here?'

He looked at his watch and shook his head. 'No, thanks. We'd better get going or we'll miss the party.'

He was driving a small, rather battered Triumph Spitfire convertible. The engine sounded like a dentist's drill, thought Claire as they screeched off towards Chalk Farm.

They parked outside the Medical School and followed the booming sound of the music.

A mad scene greeted her inside. Hordes of medical students, garlanded with streamers and pieces of tinsel, popped cork after cork of champagne.

'Good evening, *Doctor* Green,' called Bill to a small redheaded student with shaving foam all over her fringe, and she shrieked with laughter.

'I still can't believe I'm qualified!' she shouted back as someone handed her a glass of champagne. 'We're sitting over by the jukebox. Join us, Bill, won't you?'

Bill nodded and took Claire's hand and led her over to a table near the door. There were about fifteen people grouped around the table.

'It's Christmas, folks, and here comes Bill with my present!' quipped a lanky aristocractic-looking man in a white coat who was drinking from a bottle of champagne.

'Shut up, Alex. This is Claire and she's with me, and I don't want you frightening her off!'

The tall man sat up elegantly. 'Scare Claire? My dear boy, I wouldn't dream of it. How do you do, Claire? The name is Alex Morris-Clarke. I can tell that this philistine won't dream of introducing us for fear that I'll tempt you away. Now, come and sit by me and tell me your life story.'

Giggling, and shrugging off Bill's disgruntled expression, Claire perched on the seat beside Alex and was immediately handed the champagne bottle.

'Drink to me only with thine eyes,
And I will pledge with mine,' said Alex, winking at her. He turned to Bill. 'And stop glaring at me, will you, Dixon? I'm only showing the wee lassie a bit of hospitality!'

The evening carried on in much the same vein. Claire had never seen so much alcohol consumed at one sitting. She told Bill and Alex all about leaving modelling for nursing. She made no mention of her mentor, however.

'Modelling's loss is St Anthony's gain,' hiccuped Bill as he threw a peanut up into the air and failed to catch it in his mouth.

It transpired that Alex was the leading light of the hospital dramatic society and that the newly-qualified doctors would be staging a traditionally 'impromptu' revue that Friday.

On her fourth glass of champagne, and feeling as free as a bird, Claire found herself agreeing to take a small part and gave Alex her phone number.

Several people had fallen asleep round the table and the redheaded Dr Green was softly snoring, her head on Bill's lap. Alex had disappeared. Claire took another swig from the bottle.

Someone sat down beside her and took the bottle from her hand.

'You give that back!' she demanded indignantly, and found herself looking into a pair of very familiar eyes. 'Luke!' she exclaimed.

'I'm surprised that you can still recognise me,' he said gravely, trying to bite a smile back.

'Of course I can recognise you,' she said crossly.

'Give me some more champagne—I'm thirsty!'

He put it to his lips and took a mouthful, then pulled a face and placed it on the table in front of them, taking great care not to disturb the pyramid of empty lager cans which somebody had erected there.

'It's flat and it's warm. I can't think of anything worse to drink. You're tipsy, Claire. And I'll bet you haven't eaten anything.'

'Oh yes, I have,' she told him, putting on the most dignified voice she could. 'I've had fourteen peanuts and four cheese sticks—I know, because Alex and I counted them out.'

Luke frowned. 'Who brought you here tonight?'

Bill sat up with an effort. 'Hello, Luke.' He grinned foolishly. 'Don't worry about Claire. I'll drive her home in a minute.'

'You're in no state to drive anywhere, Bill. I should stoke up on black coffee and sleep in the hospital tonight. Come on, Claire, I'm taking you home.'

Claire opened her mouth to protest, but when she saw the expression on Luke's fce, she shut it again. 'Yes, m'lud,' she giggled as he took her arm and guided her out of the bar.

There was no motorbike tonight. Instead there was the sleek saloon he had told her about. 'And where's Jilly?' she demanded, as he held the door open for her.

'Oh, she's at home,' he replied vaguely. There was a pulse beating insistently at his temple. She was in a very dangerous mood tonight. He would have to go carefully.

He drove quickly and in silence, broken only by Claire attempting once to sing, 'Show me the way to go home'. Luke drew up outside her flat and walked round to the passenger door to let her out. Her head was resting against her shoulders, curls falling down her back. He shook her gently.

'Come on, sweetheart—nearly home.'

She shook her head a little and let him help her out of the car. Was she dreaming, or had he really called her 'sweetheart'?

He took the key from her and opening the main door led her up the steps to her flat. He unlocked the door and they stood there for a moment, in silence.

'Do you want me to come in and make you some coffee?' he asked.

Claire shook her head, bright curls flying. 'Nope.' Her face was very close to his. 'There's only one thing I want.'

He shouldn't ask it. He *shouldn't* ask it. Even as he thought it, he heard himself saying, 'And what's that?'

'This.' She framed his face with her hands and leant forward and softly kissed him.

For a moment Luke stiffened. For a moment he kissed her back. How did the old song go—kisses sweeter than wine? He wanted her so badly.

Gently, very gently, he disentangled her from him, and pushed her through the door.

'Goodnight, Claire,' he whispered as he shut it behind her and began to walk slowly back down the stairs.

CHAPTER EIGHT

THE ALARM CLOCK shrilled noisily and Claire opened her eyes. She registered that it was six-thirty and was just about to snuggle down underneath the duvet for five more minutes, when the events of the previous evening came flooding back, and she sat up quickly in horror, then wished she hadn't as her head began to spin.

How could she? How could she have done such a thing? She might have been flippant with Luke in the bar, and on the journey home—but that had nothing on her behaviour when they reached her flat.

Her cheeks burned scarlet as she remembered what she'd said, her tongue loosened by the champagne. And then to lean forward and kiss him like that. What must he think? She'd even asked him about Jilly French. What had he said? 'Oh, she's at home.'

What had she expected him to say? To deny all knowledge of Jilly when they'd been sitting conspiratorially close together in the library?

With an aching head and stiff limbs she walked into the kitchen and made herself a cup of strong black coffee. She drank it in the bedroom as she pulled on her uniform and rubbed hard at her cheeks, trying to bring a little colour back into them.

What had she promised herself just twenty-four hours previously? That she was going to put Luke out of her mind once and for all. Previous promises had included not becoming a nuisance or behaving like a love-struck schoolgirl. So how would she describe kissing him out of the blue?

Despite her shame and her self-reproachment, she couldn't suppress a shudder of longing as she remembered the kiss. For a few moments it had been pure, undiluted bliss, until he had propelled her into the flat, as you would an over-enthusiastic puppy who was jumping up with muddy paws.

How could she possibly face him again? She buttoned up her gaberdine and ran downstairs to the hall to unlock her bicycle.

There was a strong smell of freshly ground coffee as she cycled past the small health-food restaurant in Primrose Hill Road, and for a moment she could have imagined she was in Paris. She glumly wished she *was* in Paris.

She arrived on the ward promptly at seven-thirty and, for once, there seemed to be enough staff. Sister was in charge and Claire was paired to work with Staff Nurse Lee. To her enormous relief, Jilly French was off for two days. She would have hated to have faced her this morning. What if Luke had gone back to her last night and told her of Claire's fumbling attempts at seduction?

Nurse Lee's forthcoming wedding to Nigel was due to take place in a fortnight's time, and at every available moment she talked of nothing else.

'I couldn't decide whether to have carnations or roses for the buttonholes,' she babbled excitedly, as she deftly folded a neat envelope corner at the bottom of the counterpane. 'Well, my mother wanted us to have yellow roses, like she and Daddy did. But you'll never guess what?' She was looking at Claire expectantly.

'No, what?' Claire answered hurriedly, wishing her head would stop hurting.

'If you want yellow roses, they have to be imported from Holland—and they end up costing *twice* as much!' Nurse Lee finished triumphantly, and moved on to the next bed.

At the end of report, Sister mentioned Mr Lewis.

'This was our young man who had a massive GI bleed the other day. He was transferred to Intensive Care, where Dr Stellingworth's team stabilised him, and performed endoscopy. He was then handed over to the surgeons, and his duodenal ulcer operated on, and he's doing very nicely now.'

So Luke's diagnosis of duodenal ulcer had been correct, thought Claire.

'I'd just like to say,' added Sister, 'that Mr Lewis had a very large and very frightening bleed while Nurse Scott was temporarily alone on the ward. She acted very quickly and very efficiently, and I'm especially proud of her.' Claire went pink with embarrassment and pleasure.

Sister turned to look at all the girls clustered in a circle around the small office, all with their different faces, their different coloured belts. She smiled.

'I wanted to say that because, as I think most of you know, I don't believe that nurses get the thanks they deserve, particularly from within the profession itself.' She began to close the Kardex. 'Anyway, having got all that off my chest, it's back to work, please, girls!'

They all laughed and pushed the chairs back against the walls. As Claire accompanied Ella Lee on the drug round, she thought how decent it had been of Sister to compliment her in front of all the others.

She was a genuinely kind woman, and a very perceptive one too. Claire was aware that she had been wearing a long face all morning, and that there was really no need for it. She must not bring her personal life to work.

She knew in her heart of hearts that she had the makings of a good nurse, and she was not going to let anyone spoil that, least of all herself. She would be even better, and she would last the course, and qualify. And prove all the Doubting Thomases wrong.

She went to the canteen for her break with Staff Nurse Lee, where she drank more strong coffee and ate a bowl of cornflakes, and immediately felt better.

'Late night?' asked her companion smugly, but didn't bother waiting for a reply. 'I'm always in bed by ten when I'm on an early. I send Nigel home.'

Poor Nigel, thought Claire, but didn't say anything.

When they got back to the ward, Sister left Staff Nurse Lee in charge and Claire was left to do the four-hourly temperature, pulses and respirations, or TPRs as they were known, while Anna Hunter tackled a particularly nasty dressing.

Claire was on the second to last bed when Staff came out of the office, waving her hands in the air as she always did if the ward did not swing to a precise routine.

'There's a diabetic keto-acidosis on its way up from Cas,' she explained, her small eyes darting from side to side in her face. 'We'll have to move Mr Ronaldson down and bring the empty bed up next to the office. After that, we've no more beds, thank goodness.'

They moved the bed and Claire quickly washed it down with antiseptic before calling her senior to help her make it up.

'Then can you get TPR charts, and a fluid chart? One of the doctors will be coming up with the patient to start an IVI, so make sure you've got a drip stand next to the bed and a litre of normal saline, as well as the usual cannulas and tape.' She looked at Claire. 'Do you think you can do all that?'

Claire nodded and went off to get all that was needed. She had helped Luke set up an infusion the other day, and so the requirements were still fresh in her mind. As her hand reached out automatically and neatly filled the kidney dish, she wondered whether it would be Luke who would be accompanying the patient. She prayed it wouldn't be. She couldn't bear to face him after her behaviour last night.

She needn't have worried. It was Bill Dixon who appeared with the stretcher. Claire watched while the porters lifted the patient on to the bed. Another young patient. Why had she imagined that all ill people would be over seventy?

This boy looked about her age. He lay back against the pillows, semi-conscious and breathing in a peculiar way.

'What's the matter with his breathing?' she asked, in a worried voice.

'He's over-breathing,' explained Bill. 'It's the body's way of trying to compensate for too much acid in the blood. But he should be OK when we get a drip into him, and we'll feed him some potassium later on.'

Soon Bill had sited the drip and the normal saline began to run in. Claire began to bandage his arm to a board, to keep the line patent.

After Bill had left, she tidied away the wrappings and plastic containers and dabbed some cottonwool soaked in ice water on to the boy's dry lips.

'Don't worry, Mr Ronaldson,' she told him softly. 'You're in the best possible hands now.'

It was true. She was echoing words which she had once heard Luke use.

She took the IVI chart into the office, to show Sister. Bill was sitting at the desk writing in the notes. He glanced up as Claire came in.

'He's only eighteen,' he said. 'A new diabetic. How we handle him in here will colour his attitude to his condition for the rest of his life.'

Claire nodded. 'I'll remember that.'

By the time she left the ward at four-thirty, Derek Ronaldson had already shown some improvement and sat propped up against his pillows, looking round at the ward in between closing his eyes and drifting off again.

Claire went to say goodbye to him. 'I'll see you tomorrow, Mr Ronaldson,' she whispered. 'Have a good rest.'

He mumbled something, but she couldn't make it out. She bent her head closer. This time it was clearer.

'Call me . . . Derry.'

She leaned him forward while she plumped up his pillow. 'Very well, then—Derry, but don't tell Sister!'

He managed a smile and closed his eyes again.

Claire walked briskly up the main corridor towards the changing-rooms when she heard the sound of running footsteps. Please don't let it be him, she thought, then changed her mind. Please let it be him, so that I can at least apologise.

It was Bill again. He was out of breath.

'Couldn't really speak to you on the ward. Look—I'm sorry about last night,' he said, shamefaced. 'I had rather a lot to drink. Did you get home OK?'

'Yes, I was fine,' she said hastily. 'Everyone was a bit tipsy. Please don't worry, Bill. I had a great evening. It was fun.'

She hoped that her words didn't sound insincere and hollow. It was true, she *had* had fun. Until her tongue had run away with her.

'Alex tells me you're the surprise finale in the revue. Is that true?'

She'd forgotten all about it—what *had* got into her last night? She wondered what Alex had in mind.

'He wants you to turn up backstage tomorrow, by about eight o'clock. You are going to do it, aren't you?'

Why not? She had nothing else planned. The medical students were a good laugh, and the more friends she made, the better. Maybe people of her own age would make her forget older men who made her feel stupid.

They had reached the changing-room. Claire put her hand on the discoloured brass doorknob and looked at Bill.

'Yes, of course I'm going to do it. I'll see you there.' She walked inside and unpinned her cap.

Which was how she came to be sitting in a cramped dressing-room, wearing what looked like a cross between a French maid and a nurse's outfit, listening to loud shouts and banging from the stage and the distant laughter of the audience.

She hadn't been keen on the black stockings, clearly visible beneath the short skirt, but

Alex Morris-Clarke was nothing if not gifted with a tongue of silver.

'They'll love it,' he had exclaimed excitedly. 'Everybody's fantasy nurse—but of course you'll be sending the whole idea up.'

'How?' she had asked pointedly.

'My dear,' he had said in his supercilious drawl, 'by playing the music to *The Stripper*, we'll be taking the mickey out of them all.'

An echo from her past. It was the kind of thing that she had once been paid a great deal of money for. But this was different. This time it was for a good cause. The money would be going towards kidney research.

She slipped on the high-heeled black shoes and leaned into the mirror to re-apply her lipstick.

There was a loud rap at the door and she turned and called 'Come in', thinking that it might be her cue. The door was pushed open and there stood Luke, breathing heavily, his lips tight with anger.

He slowly looked her up and down, an incredulous expression on his face. He moved towards her and she took a step back. There was something almost terrifying about his demeanour.

'What the hell is going on?' he demanded, taking hold of her elbow and staring furiously into her face.

Claire shrank away from him. 'I'm—I'm in the revue,' she stuttered. .

His face was white with rage and his eyes were blazing green fire. He had somehow managed to make every object in the room seem smaller and insignificant. She had never seen anyone look so furious.

'And why, might I ask, are you dressed up looking like some French tart?' His voice sounded ominously controlled now.

'Because that's what I'm wearing,' she answered stubbornly, meeting his eyes now. What right did he have to storm in here, demanding this and demanding that? He had made it plain that he wanted nothing to do with her.

'You most certainly are not wearing it,' he told her quietly. 'Now take it off.'

'I will not take it off!' she yelled at him. 'I don't have to do what you tell me!'

His eyes never left her face, and when he spoke his voice was harsh. 'Take it off before I rip it off.'

The grey-green eyes were like flint, and she looked into them challengingly, then smiled.

'Go on, then,' she goaded him. 'Rip it off—if you like.'

Luke suddenly felt unutterably old and weary.

'Stop it, Claire.' His voice sounded sad. 'Just get changed, will you. And don't argue. Do you want me to wait outside?'

'Yes, please,' she answered automatically, her voice that of a polite little girl. When he had gone she leaned helplessly against the door—all her strength seemed to have left her. Her eyes were stinging with unshed tears. She began to shake.

So he didn't even want her in that way. It was the ultimate rejection. She had offered him everything, and he had turned it down. She dabbed at her eyes with a crumpled, sodden tissue, but she would not give him the pleasure of seeing her cry.

It took ten minutes before she was dressed and felt calm enough to face him. He was standing directly outside the door, almost as though he were guarding it, his handsome face serious. The revue was still in progress, Claire could hear a male falsetto giving a shrill monologue.

'What about Alex?' she asked. 'What shall I tell him?'

'I've spoken to him,' Luke said baldly. 'I've explained that you won't be doing it. I told him to use one of his own girlfriends as a sex object. Come on, I'm taking you home.'

Despite her humiliation, she managed to see the irony in the situation. He always seemed to be rescuing her, delivering her home safely. That was, if he wasn't having a major effect on her life by guiding her career choice. Just what had she thought about before Luke Hayward entered her life?

'Do you want to listen to some music?' he asked as she fastened her seat belt, and she shrugged.

He put on some very loud opera, which she thought might be Wagner. It was angry and violent, and it was passionate. She was reminded of the look on Luke's face as he stormed into her dressing-room.

He stopped the car outside her flat and for a minute they sat there in silence, then Claire started to open the door.

'Aren't you going to ask me in for coffee

tonight?' he asked.

She shrugged. 'If you like.' She moved like a robot, all emotion drained from her.

Luke walked behind her up the stairs, but this time he did not close the door behind her. This time he followed her inside. It was the first time he had been there. He loved the soft yellow walls, her pictures and her furniture. Her home was as fresh and as attractive as she was.

She came back into the sitting-room from the kitchen to find him glancing at her record collection.

'Just waiting for the kettle to boil,' she said flatly. 'It's only instant, I'm afraid.'

He stood up. 'Instant's fine.'

Claire began to draw the curtains and he watched her as she smoothed their folds into place. She turned to face him, the soft light from the lamp on the table turning the apricot of her dress into a warm peach colour.

'I'm sorry,' she said, gesturing to a tray of bottles. 'Perhaps you'd prefer a drink?'

'Coffee will be fine, thanks.' He continued to wander around the room, peering at her books and her ornaments.

Just why was he here? she wondered. He had chastised her as you would a child, his anger and disgust had been plain. So what was he doing here—chatting politely and waiting for coffee?

Suddenly she asked, 'How did you know where to find me tonight?'

Luke paused in his examination of a delicate

inlaid box above the fireplace. For the first time since they had arrived back at the flat he met her eyes.

'Bill Dixon told me. He said Alex had asked you to do some spectacular finale.'

She raised her eyebrows. 'So Bill told you—just like that?'

He looked slightly uncomfortable. 'Well, no, not exactly. I had a word with him about you.'

She looked at him in amazement. 'What do you mean—you had a word with him about me? What exactly did you say? Am I allowed to know?'

Luke frowned. 'I simply told him that it wasn't on to take a girl for a drink, and then be incapable of driving her home afterwards, that's all.'

Claire turned on him. 'That's all? You say that's all?' Her voice rose in a rage. 'You've acted like some reactionary Victorian father and you say that's all? I'm not your ward, you know, Luke. I don't need a guardian angel constantly lurking in corners and extricating me from difficult situations.'

His patience finally broke. 'Well, dammit, Claire, I think you do. I can't imagine how you ever looked after yourself when you were modelling!'

She looked at him, standing so tall and so powerful in the small sitting-room.

'But why did you make such a ridiculous fuss about my costume? We're not living in the Dark Ages, you know. It was far less revealing than anything you'd see on the beach!'

'A bikini on the beach would be in context. That wasn't,' Luke snapped at her. The eyes began to grow flinty again. 'Honestly, Claire, that outfit was sheer titillation! Sexual exploitation, if you like.' The voice was angry now. 'You don't have to do that kind of thing any more.'

She was standing only a few feet away from him. 'But what I can't understand,' she persisted softly, 'is why you made me change. Even if all you say is true, why should it bother you what I do?'

There was no sound, except for the faint hissing of a kettle, a tap dripping once, twice.

Luke swallowed, and cleared his throat, to decide how to put it into words.

'Why?' Claire repeated.

He took a step forward. He knew what was about to happen and there was nothing he could do to stop it. It had been etched on the blueprint of his life; there was no point in fighting it any longer. And why else had he come here tonight, if not for this?

'Don't you know?' he asked simply. 'Oh, my darling Claire—don't you know?'

For a moment she searched his face anxiously, as if seeking the truth behind his words. Then two steps, that was all it took. Two steps and she was in his arms and he was holding her so tightly that she could scarcely draw a breath.

He put his hands in her hair, and the thick curls coiled around his fingers. The pent-up hunger which had been haunting him for weeks began to be released, as he started to cover every inch of her face with tiny kisses. Not a millimetre of skin was to escape his lips. And then he found her mouth, and he felt her lips part.

It was as though the whole of her life before had been a rehearsal for what was about to happen and her real life was about to begin. She had been a troubled raft, buffeted and marooned, safe at last on dry land.

Their clothes fell from them like autumn leaves, by whose hand she could never remember. And there, on the Persian rug, amongst the blue silk cushions, Luke Hayward made love to her.

CHAPTER NINE

WHEN LUKE AWOKE he kissed the back of her neck. 'Hello, darling,' he murmured, and then said 'darling' again, as though he had learnt a new word and couldn't repeat it too often.

He sensed, rather than heard, that Claire was crying. Her head lay cradled in the crook of his arm, her head turned away from him, and when he spoke again his voice was so soft that she had to strain her ears to hear him.

'Are you sorry it happened?'

A muffled sob. 'No.'

He turned her chin so that she was facing him. Even crying had been unable to alter her beauty. The pale cheeks were streaked with tears and her eyes glittered brightly.

With a gentle finger he wiped each tear away. 'Because it was your first time?'

So he knew that too. 'No.' She buried her head in his shoulder, in the warm nakedness of his flesh. How could she describe to him the churning conflict of feelings she had experienced since he had come to her flat that evening?

There was the ecstasy and the joy bestowed on her by his lovemaking. There could be no regrets about something which felt so right. She had longed for him, but her longing had been the nebulous dreams of a young virgin. She had not known what it was she had wanted from him.

Now she knew. She had wanted him to make her complete, and he had done so. It should have been enough, but it was not enough. She hadn't stopped to think of the consequences when she had led him on, when she had fallen eagerly into his arms. She had ruthlessly pursued the proof of her attraction to him.

But he was already involved. He had his Jilly and he was not the kind of man to practise subterfuge, and even if he had been, she could never have contemplated sharing him with another woman. So where did that leave her?

Luke pulled her over so that she lay on top of him, the snaking tendrils of her hair tickling his chin. 'Tell me,' he smiled. 'It can't be that bad, can it?'

Her mouth had begun to tremble ominously, and he kissed her firmly. 'Claire, will you stop crying and tell me what the matter is. And then we can sort it out, can't we?'

She somehow doubted it. 'It's your girlfriend,' she blurted out. 'I feel so bad now.'

A look of surprise crossed his face and she saw him frown. 'My girlfriend?' he repeated, and then a smile crossed his lips. 'Ah, yes. You probably mean Jilly, don't you?'

She nodded mutely and tried to roll off him, but he grasped her firmly.

'There are two things that you should know

about Jilly,' he said. 'The first is that she has applied to go to medical school, and I've been coaching her.' He began to rub the small of her neck and she wriggled with pleasure before pushing his hand away. She wanted to hear what else he had to say.

'The second thing is that we're soon to become relatives. Now *wait* a minute, before you start jumping to any more conclusions, and let me explain.'

'Explain, then,' she mumbled sullenly. It was even worse than she had imagined. Marriage. 'Are you getting married, then?' she asked in a tiny, scared voice.

His lips twitched with amusement and he shook his head vehemently. 'Never! But Jilly is. She's engaged to my stepbrother—Claude.'

'Your stepbrother!' She breathed a huge smile of relief. It was all right, everything was ll right. 'Claude . . . Why does that name sound familiar?' she asked him, her fingers smoothing back his rumpled hair.

'Because you almost met him. Don't you remember? The night we went to the Chestnut Tree out by Runnymede. It's Claude's restaurant, but he wasn't there. I wanted you to meet him—he's never met any of my girlfriends before, you know. And then I got cold feet—you scared me, you know—do you realise that?'

Claire was grinning so much, so happy that she felt as though she would burst with joy. There was so much she wanted to say to him, and she started with the prosaic.

'What time is it?'

Luke held his wrist up. 'Just before ten. Do you realise we've been lying on this floor for nearly two hours? By the way, do you have a bed?'

She blushed. 'Yes, of course. Do you want to go to sleep?'

He grinned wickedly. 'No, but I'd like us to go and lie down.'

She buried her face in his chest, her heart thumping with delight. 'In a minute, just let me remember this.' She lay there for a moment or two, warm and safe in the haven of his arms. She loved him so much. She wanted to tell him, except that maybe it would frighten him. She had never imagined that it could be like this.

'Are you hungry?' she whispered.

'Very,' he murmured, his mouth at the base of her throat.

'Shall I make something for us to eat?'

'Mmm.'

It was exquisite. It was almost unbearable. And afterwards he picked her up and carried her into the bedroom and covered her up with a duvet, then wrapped a towel round his waist and disappeared in the direction of the kitchen, telling her that he was going to prepare a picnic for them.

Claire snuggled back against the pillow to wait. She must have drifted off, because when she opened her eyes there stood Luke, half naked and smiling at her delightedly.

'You look like the cat who's got the cream,' he

grinned as he set a loaded tray down on the bedside table and sat on the edge of the bed.

'Not cream—you!' she answered. 'What have you brought to eat?'

They picnicked on hunks of French bread, and hummus and cheeses, with black olives and grapes. First they drank a glass of mineral water and then Luke opened a bottle of champagne.

'I hope you weren't saving this for something special,' he joked.

'Well, I was, so you'd better open it,' Claire answered shyly.

The straw-coloured fizzy liquid foamed up the side of the tall, tulip-shaped glasses, and there was a resonant bell-like ring as they touched them in a toast.

'What are you working tomorrow?' asked Luke.

'It's Saturday, isn't it? I'm on a late duty, followed by an early on Sunday.'

'Bloody unsocial hours,' he grumbled, then turned to look at her. He was in the bed of this lovely young girl, drinking champagne, and the way she was looking at him was making him want her all over again. He pushed the nagging doubts to the back of his mind and reached for her.

Just before he kissed her, she remembered, and when she spoke her voice was serious. 'When do you leave for Glasgow?'

He wished she hadn't mentioned it. 'In just over three weeks, but don't let's think about it,' he told her, his lips brushing against hers tantalisingly softly.

'I'll try,' she promised, and presently the joy of

their passion pushed it firmly to the back of their minds.

But it hovered there, like an evil black cloud, waiting to descend and suffocate them.

CHAPTER TEN

IT WAS like playing at being married. The following morning Claire turned lazily to find Luke's warm flesh against hers and his arms around her waist, and in a delicious state of half-sleepiness, he began to make love to her again.

Afterwards they ate breakfast, sitting opposite each other in the kitchen, brilliant sunshine streaming across the table. They heated up the rest of the French bread and spread it with great golden pats of butter and some dark, rich black cherry jam which Claire had brought back from one of her last trips to France. They dunked the bread into huge cups of fresh coffee and munched it noisily, laughing as the crumbs spread around their elbows.

'Tell me,' he chuckled, as he watched her break off another huge chunk of bread, 'is it mandatory to make as much mess as possible?'

'Oh, absolutely,' she replied, licking some of the jam from the edge of her mouth. 'The French do it all the time, don't they?'

He was quiet for a moment. 'Yes, they do.' Then, 'My mother is married to a Frenchman.'

He didn't sound very happy about it, thought Claire, watching him closely.

He looked up to meet her eyes. 'What are you

thinking?' he asked softly.

They had not been easy thoughts. 'I was thinking that really I know absolutely nothing about you.'

Luke took her hand to his lips and kissed it. 'Yes, you do. You know all the most important things.' But he could see a faint look of concern remaining.

'What exactly do you want to know?' He found himself staring at her long brown legs.

'Everything. I want to know absolutely everything!'

He smiled indulgently. She was still such a child—so straightforward, and so heartbreakingly honest. She had obviously never played the morning-after game before. The light, teasing comments. The superficial remarks belonging to the casual affair.

'I shall tell you everything—well, everything that I want you to know!' he teased her. 'But not today. It will never be as magical as this again, so let's not waste it. Come here.'

She was his willing slave. She walked round the table and sat on his lap, her arms around his neck. And as he led her back to the bedroom, she thought wildly that she had found paradise.

He dropped her off in time for her late duty, and kissed her soundly.

'I'll pick you up here later,' he told her. 'What time do you finish?'

'Nine-thirty,' she replied, thinking he looked a little irritated.

'It's a ridiculous time to finish,' he began, then stopped when he saw the look on her face. 'I'm sorry, darling—I didn't mean to moan. I'd just have liked us to have a long evening together, that's all. Never mind, don't have any supper in the canteen, and I'll make something for us.'

'OK.' She gave him a hurried final kiss and hurried away through the swing doors.

Luke sat there in the car for a few minutes after she had gone. What had he started? Where was it going to lead? He turned the key in the ignition and revved the engine angrily. He should have resisted her. He had known what would happen and he had set himself up for it. He had had only a few weeks remaining and he had been unable to keep away from her.

But it was too late now to start thinking about what he should or shouldn't have done. He must enjoy what they had, and let the future sort itself out.

But even as he drove away, he felt a great churning mixture of desire and fear eating away at his insides.

Claire arrived on the ward ten minutes before her duty started and took the opportunity to tiptoe down to Derry Ronaldson's bed. He was sitting up in bed, his fair wavy hair neatly brushed and clad in his own pyjamas instead of the thin white hospital gown he had worn on admission to the ward. He smiled when he saw her.

He looked so much better, thought Claire as she walked over to him. Not yet one hundred per cent, but a lot better.

'Hello, gorgeous,' he said, and winked.

She waggled a finger at him. 'I can see you're

feeling *much* better!'

'Give me another day and I'll be ready to chase you nurses around the ward.'

She laughed. 'We're all Olympic champions on this ward!' She picked up his fluid chart and peered at it. 'Still got the drip up, then, Derry?'

He grimaced. 'Yeah, Doctor says I'll have it for about three days.'

She slotted the chart back into its holder at the bottom of the bed. 'Are you eating anything yet?'

'A bit. Don't really feel like much at the moment.'

She caught sight of the ward clock. 'Gracious! I'd better go into the office for report, before Sister comes yelling for me!'

He grinned. 'This Sister of yours sounds a right ogre—does she do anything other than tell you nurses off all day?'

'No,' she answered, chuckling. 'That's what Sisters are for.'

She joined the others in the office. She felt wonderful—almost euphoric. She must try to calm down.

The atmosphere on the evening duty was entirely different from an early. The mornings were one constant chase to get everything done on time. It was difficult to get twenty-eight patients bathed or washed by ten-thirty, and then make all their beds.

But by lunchtime, when the evening shift began, most of the patients were settled in bed for an afternoon rest and there was an overlap of staff until the morning shift went home at four-thirty.

This left three or sometimes four nurses on duty,

to give out medicines, suppers and get the patients ready for bed. This as well as all the usual TPRs, checking of charts, giving out bedpans, pouring out drinks or any of the many small jobs which always needed doing.

An evening duty at the weekend was the quietest of all, since all the main hospital departments were closed to all but emergencies. This meant that there were no routine X-rays, or physiotherapy. No pharmacists or social workers coming to the wards, and no grand ward rounds which necessitated the collation of charts and Sister hurrying round to see that everything was up to date.

After she had run through the latest developments on the ward, Sister allocated the weekend work. These were jobs which could only be done at the weekend, when the ward was quiet.

Anna Hunter and Nurse Goldsmith were given ward cleaning and ordering to do. After they had thoroughly cleaned every inch of the sluice room and the clinic-room, they would make certain that the ward was well stocked with needles, dressings and infusions.

Sister was to examine the drug trolley, to see if there were any shortages of medicines, and to return to Pharmacy any that were past the date on the label.

Claire was given the weekly urine to check. Twenty-eight small bottles lay in the sluice, awaiting the dipstick which would show the presence of any sugar, protein or ketones.

Mrs Haynes had explained to them the importance of urine testing. 'It's often the first physical sign of illness which is detected, and it must therefore be looked at properly. Look at it as you would a wine, girls.' She had smiled gently as they shrieked their horror.

'I'm serious,' she had continued. 'Before you use the dipstick, you should check the urine for colour and smell. The nurse's eyes and nose can be two of her most valuable assets.'

Claire remembered her words as she surveyed the bottles in front of her. The routine urine testing was not the most popular of jobs, but it was one she was thankful to have been given today. At least it had brought her down to earth!

She felt she needed a little time to calm down, after what had happened to her last night. It was silly, and it was corny, but she did feel like a different young woman from the one who had left work yesterday afternoon.

She had grown up. Love was no longer a mystery to her. She was lucky to have found someone like Luke to love.

She unlocked the small white cupboard which contained all the testing materials, including the special tablets which could accurately pinpoint the percentage of sugar in a diabetic's urine.

As she began testing, she frowned. Love. Luke had not mentioned love to her. He had told her she was beautiful, adorable. He had called her 'sweetheart', 'darling' and 'angel', but he had left out any reference to that tiny word she had been longing to say to him.

But what did she expect? A proposal of marriage

after the first kiss?

The intensity and ferocity of the passion with which she had responded to Luke's lovemaking had startled her. She had only been kissed by about half a dozen men before Luke, and nothing more than a kiss. The practised passes or tentative fumblings of the men who had kissed her had always been repulsed. They had left her cold.

Often, in her bed at night, she had wondered if she were capable of arousal, if she would ever be able to receive and to give love.

Well, last night had certainly disproved her fears. He had laughed with joy, had mocked her, then teased her and tantalised her. And then made love to her all over again. And yet he had known that there had been no other, had been gentle and tender.

It had been a night for rapture, and tears. But what was it he had said which had caused her to shiver with fear? 'It will never be as magical as this again.' Those had been his words. What could he have meant? It had struck her as a very cynical remark. It had the chilling ring of an epitaph about it.

The sound of the phone ringing broke into her thoughts and she mentally reprimanded herself. They were both single. He had no long-standing girlfriend. She would just have to be patient. If only he wasn't due to go off to Glasgow!

But he was. In just over three weeks he would be gone. Claire held a dipstick up next to the chart on the bottle and watched as the squares turned pale green.

Just because he was leaving St Anthony's it did not necessarily mean that the affair would be over. Please.

She calmed down a bit after that, and weighed most of the patients and then checked everybody's blood pressure.

At teatime she went down to the canteen, where she spotted Mary sitting on her own. She carried over a ham sandwich and a large currant bun covered with bright pink icing, and Mary wrinkled up her nose. 'You'll get fat,' she warned.

'No, I won't,' answered Claire, through a mouthful of crumbs. 'Belton's far too busy, and besides, I've had nothing since breakfast. How's life on Female Surgical?'

Mary pulled a face. 'Busy. Predictable. The women do nothing but moan. I'm looking forward to a change. Did you know that the change list is up?'

Claire looked up, her bun halfway to her mouth. 'No. No, I didn't.' The change list was displayed on a notice board in the Nurses' Home and indicated which ward each student nurse would be going to next. 'Did you notice where I'm going?'

Mary smiled. 'Yes, I did. We're nearly doing a swop—you're going to Bluebell and I'm going to Casualty—whoopee!'

'You lucky thing! Casualty seems to be everybody's favourite choice—what's Bluebell like?'

Mary spluttered into her tea-cup.

'Well, I don't want to put you off, so the less said about Sister Fulton the better. She's currently after the Surgical Registrar and not making much headway. She'll definitely not warm to someone like you joining the staff.'

Claire shrugged. 'She needn't worry about me. By the way, how's our mutual friend Simon Saunders?'

Mary immediately began to dimple. 'Oh, he's fine. Great, in fact. He took me to a Tchaikovsky evening at the Albert Hall last night—it was wonderful. Do you know, I'd never been there before.'

Claire looked surprised. 'Tchaikovsky? I didn't know Simon was a music buff.'

Her friend was smiling smugly. 'He's a surprising man.' She moved her head closer to Claire's and lowered her voice. 'Don't tell anyone, but he's asked me to move in with him.' She glanced at Claire to see her reaction.

Claire's eyes were like saucers. 'So soon? I don't believe it! He *must* be smitten—he's the world's perpetual bachelor, you know! Are you going to?'

Mary ran the tip of her finger round and round the rim of her tea-cup. 'I think so,' she answered quietly, and there was a radiant look about her. 'I think it's for keeps.'

Claire looked down. She was pleased for her friend, but it brought it slamming home how insecure her own romantic future lay.

'And how about you?' asked Mary. 'Anything new in the love line?'

Claire shook her head. She didn't want to say anything just yet—not even to Mary. 'I haven't got time to think of men,' she joked, and stood up, brushing the crumbs from her uniform.

'By the way, I meant to ask—how did the finals

party go the other evening? Anyone interesting there?' asked Mary.

'No, not really,' replied Claire vaguely. 'But it was fun all the same. Everyone had far too much champagne to drink, including myself! I'd better get back now.'

Mary stood up too. 'So must I. Why don't we go out for a drink together one night? I could ask Simon to bring someone to make up a foursome, if you like. Or we could go out, just the two of us?'

'No blind dates, please!' laughed Claire. 'You and I will paint the town red together one evening.'

They parted, promising to meet up soon, and as Claire made her way back to Belton, she wondered why she had been so secretive about Luke, particularly when Mary had herself been so confiding. It was as though she was being superstitious—if she told anyone else then it might break the spell. She didn't want other people knowing. She didn't want outside forces and hospital gossip placing any stress on their last three weeks.

That evening Luke met her in the car park and she hurled herself into his arms as though she had not seen him for a week.

And later, as she sat curled up in his shirt, watching him grill steaks and crush garlic into the salad dressing, she wondered why she persisted in thinking of them as their *last* weeks together.

CHAPTER ELEVEN

WHEN CLAIRE was to look back, those three weeks were invariably bittersweet, as the days ticked by and became weeks. She loved her job very much, but she loved Luke more, and she didn't have him for very much longer. And so it took every vestige of concentration she had to work hard and not to keep thinking of him.

They spent every spare minute together. If she was on an early, they would sometimes travel up to the West End to see a show. Once, Luke took her ice-skating at Richmond and they teetered around on the narrow blades, falling in each other's arms on to the cold ice.

Afterwards he had bought her hot chocolate, laced with rum and topped with whipped cream and grated chocolate. They had watched the sun setting over the same silvery ribbon winding up to the city which Turner had once immortalised.

He was delighted to discover that Claire really *did* enjoy riding pillion on his motorbike, and on the long summer evenings they drove out as far as they could before the light faded. Out through tree-lined, sun-dappled country lanes, the sweet smell of hay wafting across the harvested fields.

They would stop at some small pub on the way

back, drinking lager and eating giant sausages with fiery mustard. And they would laugh like schoolchildren as they kissed in shadowed car parks, before roaring back to London.

Once they drove down to the coast, in time to watch a millpond sea swallow the crimson sun. The distant Downs were bathed in fire, and Claire smelt the salty tang of the sea and felt Luke's strong, lean body next to hers and wished the evening would never end.

They both loved the fresh air and they walked often on the Heath, where the summer leaves appeared acid green against a sky of speedwell. Once they found a sheltered glade, and they made love with a desperate urgency which added a new and piquant dimension to their relationship.

Often they would just sit at home in her flat, listening to music, and staring dreamily into space—both resolutely avoiding any mention of the future.

Claire became used to Luke studying in the evening.

'Medicine is as cut-throat as the world of finance,' he told her. 'If you don't keep up to date with reading and be prepared to publish, then there's always someone waiting in the wings who is.' His face had an infectious enthusiasm about it, and she had realised how much his profession meant to him.

'There are fewer consultancy jobs than there are people applying for them. That's why I've been especially fortunate getting Professor Hempstock's job.'

She held her breath and said nothing. It was the first mention he had made of the job.

'I want to be a good doctor, Claire,' he had told her passionately, and his face became alive and enthusiastic as he spoke, his long, strong fingers smoothing back the curls from her forehead. 'Professor Hempstock has been a pioneer in his field. Getting the post of Senior Registrar on his team has been like the jewel in the crown for me. But I'll have to work like a slave—the man is an absolute workaholic and expects all his staff to be the same.' He had paused and kissed the tip of her nose, and she had been unable to dismiss the uncertainty she felt. Sometimes when he spoke about his work, she became aware of a great distance between them. He retreated from her, as he had done that time in the restaurant. She knew how excited he was about his new job, and soon she would be excluded from his daily life. Would their affair survive?

'I'm afraid we won't be able to see as much of each other as we have been, my love.' His voice was soft in her ear.

The untroubled smile which greeted this last remark owed itself to her model training, and did nothing to betray the dread which she experienced whenever she thought of him going.

He had said nothing of his feelings for her and she had not liked to ask. What on earth could she say, in any case? 'Do you love me, Luke?' or 'What are your intentions towards me, Luke?' not only sounded positively archaic, but would probably scare him half to death.

No, they had the basis of a sound relationship, but she must not rush things. If they were meant to be, then they would be able to survive a geographical distance. It wasn't as though he was emigrating to Canada!

He took pains to avoid her on the ward, but often she would catch a glimpse of him as he did his ward round, trailed by Bill Dixon and various medical students. And she would feel a thrill of desire and pride, that she was the lover of this brilliant, handsome man.

Just once she bumped into him—literally. She was in the clinic-room, taking a dressing pack out of the cupboard, and he had come in unexpectedly. Claire whirled round against his chest, and when she saw the expression in his eyes she blushed.

'I'd better leave immediately,' he murmured, giving her the benefit of one of his wickedest grins. 'Before I do something that would be *very* unprofessional!' And Claire had turned an even deeper red as she had placed a bottle of Eusol on to the trolley.

On the few occasions when she had spent the night in his hospital flat, she had been astonished at the amount of journals and textbooks he owned. The table had been covered with reams and reams of paper, including a sheaf of closely typed sheets which, he had explained, he was hoping to submit to the *New English Journal of Medicine*.

The room was impersonal, it was not a home, and she commented on this. 'I'll only make one home,' Luke had replied, and then he said, almost as an afterthought, 'I had enough homes as a child to last me for most of my adult life.'

He hardly ever mentioned his childhood, and when he did she sensed disquiet, and an obvious reluctance to discuss it. All she knew was that his parents had gone through a fairly messy divorce with custody battles, and that his father had died just a year ago.

And all too soon it was his last week, and then his last working day. His last Sunday was to be spent travelling to Glasgow and settling in.

Claire was off on the Saturday and they spent a lazy day together. At about five Luke went back to his flat to change, and he told her to dress up and that he would pick her up just after seven.

'Where are we going?' she had asked him, and he had smiled that crooked grin of his.

'Surprise!' he teased, tapping her on the nose with his forefinger. 'Just be ready on time.'

He gave her a long, luxurious kiss and then pulled himself away from her with an effort. 'I must go and finish packing,' he said, and disappeared through the front door.

Claire heard the roar of his motorbike as she began to fill the bath. He was going to leave a huge empty void in her life. They had spent every moment they could together. What on earth would she find to do next week?

She squirted bubble-bath into the water and climbed into the fragrant foam. She watched the steam gradually obscure the mirror, and an unnatural silence fell over the flat.

She was obsessed by Luke. She wondered if it was

because she had never known another lover that she found it hard to think of anything else. All she wanted was to feel his body close to hers, to see that look of desire in his eyes, and to feel those strong hands running lazily over her body, transporting her to a different planet.

She could not decide what to wear. As she had on their first date, she tried on outfit after outfit, until the bed was piled high with discarded dresses.

She would have loved to have worn the pale silk tulle she had bought and lost that day—it seemed such a long time ago now. She had been back to the shop, thinking that perhaps someone might have found the carrier bag and handed it in, but they had received nothing. Luke had suggested she buy another like it, but it had been a one-off—she would never find another dress like it.

Eventually she decided on a short suit in electric blue taffeta, which intensified the colour of her eyes and contrasted brilliantly with her bright hair. She applied more make-up than usual, idly wondering, as she lined her eyes with a sooty blue kohl pencil, if she was perhaps sheltering behind a mask. She brushed the merest touch of silver-flecked blusher on to her cheekbones and tied her hair back with a demure velvet ribbon of exactly the same blue as the dress.

She eyed herself critically in the tall mirror in the bedroom, looking at herself with a model's professional eye. She hardly ever pulled all the stops out these days, there just hadn't seemed to be a need for it since she began nursing, but she wanted Luke to see her at her very best.

He arrived promptly at seven, his head and shoulders almost completely hidden by an enormous spray of blood-red roses. Claire took them and smelt them, they were exquisite to behold, but they were the carefully cultivated variety and had no scent. She shivered a little, hoping that it wasn't a bad omen.

She arranged them carefully in a crystal vase and put them on the table beside her bed. It was the first time that he had bought her flowers.

When she had finished she turned round to find him watching her closely. He held his arms out and she ran into them.

'You're so beautiful,' he whispered. 'But so sad. Don't be sad tonight, my love.'

'I'll try,' she promised, but her words lacked conviction.

She collected her bag and they walked hand in hand downstairs. She had known that Luke would bring the car tonight, but she stupidly felt a pang that it was not the bike. And she knew where they were going even before he headed towards Hammersmith and crossed the bridge.

They were a couple now; Claire felt grown-up and fulfilled. They sat, well dressed and neatly groomed, an attractive pair in Luke's sleek car, listening to the Rolling Stones and casting each other their secret looks.

Then why was it that all she could think of was how she had clung to him, windswept and half deafened by the powerful roar of his motorbike—her cheek against rough leather. They had been carefree then.

The dark cloud was threatening to descend. They

passed the same green expanse at Runnymede where fields became trees, behind which lay Windsor.

Luke turned to look at her and smiled. 'Nearly there. Remember this place?'

'Yes,' she replied softly.

Tonight he wore an immaculately cut suit of navy blue and with it a thin blue and white pinstripe shirt. Claire noticed that the tie was silk and the cuff-links a pale gold.

The look was expensive and dashing, but it was a side of him which she had never seen before. Even on their trips to the theatre he had worn casual trousers and a sports jacket, but he was happiest in faded jeans and heavy cotton shirts. It was strange to see him looking the epitome of sartorial elegance. The whole outfit matched perfectly, but somehow she couldn't imagine Luke going from shop to shop to find the exact shade of tie. Perhaps someone had helped him.

He glanced at her. 'What are you thinking?'

He disliked being fobbed off, that much she knew. 'How smart you look.'

He looked pleased. 'And?'

So perceptive! 'Wondering if you chose your suit and tie yourself.'

He smirked with delight. 'Jealous minx, aren't you, Miss Scott? My mother, actually.'

As he helped her out of the car she couldn't help laughing. He was right, she *was* jealous. Ridiculously jealous, really. But even so, she felt elated that an ex-girlfriend hadn't been a guiding hand in his choice of wardrobe.

Tonight he took her up a further flight of stairs to where they'd drunk on the balcony last time.

'We're dining with Claude, but upstairs in his flat, not the restaurant,' he told her.

For a moment Claire felt a brief wave of disappointment. She had hoped that their last evening would be spent alone. Perhaps he was afraid that she might become maudlin. And she was longing to meet his French stepbrother.

The door was opened by a tall, olive-skinned man with dark hair and slanting brown eyes, who looked so typically French that Claire almost giggled.

The two brothers embraced, and then the Frenchman put both hands on Claire's shoulders and looked her up and down critically for a moment.

Then he kissed her on each cheek and grasped Luke's hand, chuckling and saying, '*J'ai toujours su que tu avais du goût*!' The two men laughed, and then Claire heard a soft familiar voice calling, 'Claude!' and there, walking towards them, was Jilly French.

She had only seen Jilly out of uniform once, when she'd been dining with Luke, and she immediately wished she hadn't worn quite so much make-up.

Jilly wore a simple cream-coloured dress, but Claire knew immediately that it was haute couture. Her only jewellery was tiny pearl studs in her ears. The ash-blonde hair was cut into a new chic bob and the lazy grey eyes carried only the slightest hint of eye-shadow. Claire felt like a circus clown in comparison. She hadn't seen Jilly for almost a month, as she had left Belton.

Then Jilly turned to her with a sweet smile and said, 'We're so glad you could come, Claire. Let's go and sit down and the men can find us something to drink.'

And Claire looked up to see Luke gazing at her with such a look of longing and tenderness, which said more than a million words of love could ever have done. She knew then that she must just relax and enjoy the evening, and get to know his family properly.

She answered Jilly happily. 'That would be lovely. My throat feels like the Sahara!'

Claude began expostulating at this, holding his hands up in a bemused manner and demanding, '*Qu'est-ce qu'elle a dit*?'

'Claude speaks the most perfect English, Claire, on no account let him fool you with his poor helpless Frenchman act!'

Laughing, they all followed Jilly into the sitting-room, a grand high-ceilinged room of crimson and gold which enjoyed a breathtaking view of the Thames. There was champagne cooling in the ice-bucket, and they all drank each other's health.

'Jilly starts medical school next month,' explained Luke.

'Congratulations,' said Claire. 'Which medical school?'

'Southampton,' she replied. 'That's not too far from my darling fiancé, at least by car on the motorway. And anyway, I'm tired of London.'

' "When a man is tired of London, he is tired of life," ' quoted Luke thoughtfully.

'Well, I'm a woman, so it's different!' retorted Jilly. 'And anyway, you're a fine one to talk—you're leaving London tomorrow!'

'Ah, but I'm definitely not tired of it,' said Luke meaningfully, his eyes never leaving Claire's face.

The meal, which was sent up from the main restaurant, was delicious. They began with a spinach soufflé which was a pretty green colour, served with a creamy anchovy sauce. The main course was smoked duck breasts with a ginger butter sauce, and Claude beamed modestly as they heaped praise on him. The pudding was a simple but light-as-air *tarte au citron*, to which Claire could hardly do justice.

She found it fascinating to watch the brothers together, with Luke using his hands to illustrate a point and occasionally breaking into perfect French for some good-hearted banter with his brother, although this was quickly quashed by Jilly, who claimed it was unfair, since she and Claire couldn't understand when they spoke so quickly!

All in all, it was one of the most pleasant evenings Claire had ever spent. Claude and Jilly were the most marvellous hosts, and Luke would blow her a kiss from time to time, and his hand would rest on top of hers.

At one point, just before they were leaving when Jilly was showing Claire round the rest of the flat, she stopped with a hand on her arm and said in her low voice, 'Luke looks so very happy tonight. I do hope things work out for you both.'

'Thank you,' answered Claire. 'I hope so too. Will you be back to St Anthony's at all?'

The other girl shook her head. 'We're having a holiday and then I start at Southampton. I'm hoping that you'll be at our wedding, though. April in Paris—do you think you could bear that?'

Claire burst into a peal of laughter. 'Oh, I think I probably could!'

The two men came out of the sitting-room. 'I think we must be making tracks, Claire,' said Luke.

'Oh, but it is early!' argued Claude.

'I think they probably want to be on their own, darling,' frowned Jilly.

The Frenchman suddenly flashed her a look of comprehension.

'*D'accord, d'accord*,' he nodded, and disappeared to find Claire's handbag.

They said affectionate goodbyes and the engaged couple stood by their front door, waving until Claire and Luke had retreated out of sight.

Outside, the moon looked like a silver lantern in a starry sky and the dappled water of the river was flecked with light. The air was as warm as daytime.

Luke took Claire by the arm and they crossed the road until they stood by the edge of the bank, listening to the water as it lapped up by their feet. She stood absolutely still, afraid to move, or even to breathe, lest she break the spell.

He stood looking at her bright eyes, her hair neatly smoothed back for once. At last he spoke, and when he did his voice was gruff.

'Come here.' She stepped obediently into his arms and he began to stroke her hair. He loved to play with her hair and would spend hours in the evening, with her sitting at his feet, twisting and unfurling each strand as he read a textbook. The curls began to fall out from the ribbon, one by one.

He lifted her chin and looked down at her. 'I've had a wonderful evening, Claire. I want you to know that this past month has been one of the happiest times of my life.'

She waited to hear the rest, wondering why it sounded awfully like a dismissal.

'And of course we'll carry on seeing each other, though it's not going to be easy—with your hours and my being on call so much.'

'I know.' She gazed at his mesmeric eyes, so grey tonight, wanting to lock the memory of them firmly away for ever.

'I want you to know . . .' his voice faltered a little. 'You mean so much to me, Claire, but . . .'

'Luke . . .'

He shushed her gently. 'Listen, my darling. You're still so very young. You've your whole life in front of you, and it *has* only been a month. We must neither of us make any promises which we may not be able to keep. Do you understand?'

She nodded numbly.

He bent his head close and whispered in her ear, 'And now I'm going to drive you home as fast as is allowed by law.'

She smiled up at him, in spite of her sadness. 'And why is that?'

His eyes were glinting as he whispered something even more softly, before taking her by the hand. It was incredible—this girl made him feel about nineteen again, except that he couldn't ever remember it being as good as this when he was nineteen.

They roared away, tail lights flashing, and Claire's blue velvet ribbon lay on the riverbank, curling like a snake, discarded.

By morning, the hothouse roses had already wilted, their heads flopped down on their stems, like neglected marionettes. Claire remembered reading somewhere that they revived if you stuck a pin in them, but she had no intention of spending the morning stabbing roses.

For once, she cooked Luke breakfast. Usually they ate Continental syle, either bread or croissants warmed in the oven with different jams, or *confitures* as he called them. But today she grilled bacon and sausages, tomatoes and mushrooms and then fried eggs.

It was a disaster. The bacon was flabby and colourless—a transparent frill on the plate. The sausage was blackened and obscenely split, and the egg lay congealing in hardening fat.

Luke struggled with it valiantly for a while and eventually pushed his plate away and pulled Claire on to his lap.

'I can honestly say that was the worst breakfast I've ever had in my entire life!' He burst out laughing and she began to giggle into his shoulder, and then suddenly she was crying, great sobs making her gasp and tears wetting the front of his shirt.

'Don't, Claire.' His voice was pleading. 'Please,

darling, don't cry!'

Presently she was calm again. She lay in bed and watched him as he dressed.

'I'll just go back to the hospital, collect my things and hand in the keys.' He looked at her fondly. 'I'll ring you when I've arrived, OK?'

She nodded and managed a smile.

Somehow she saw him off. She was barefooted, wearing jeans and an old shirt. She waved until he was out of sight and stood there long after his car had disappeared until eventually a large drop of rain, quckly followed by another, reminded her where she was.

With an effort, she turned to go back inside and shivered slightly. Summer was over.

CHAPTER TWELVE

AFTER Luke had left, Claire wandered aimlessly around the flat for a while. She spent the day in a kind of daze. She found a sweater of his which he had left behind and she sat curled up on the sofa, hugging it to her, as a child would a favourite blanket, or a dog his master's slipper.

She didn't feel like eating. She switched the television on, then switched it off again. By evening, she felt freezing and put the central heating on and tried to concentrate on the Sunday papers.

Luke rang at about eight, to say that he had arrived safely and had been allocated a newly decorated hospital flat. But he sounded a long way away, and there were crackles on the line and she couldn't think of anything to say—except that she loved him. But she didn't say it. He said he would see her in a month and would ring her in the meantime.

After he had rung off, Claire replaced the receiver and sat staring at it. The reality of his absence suddenly dawned on her. She was going to have a lot of free time to fill.

The following day she was on a late duty. She walked into the office and Sister Thompson looked up from her desk and smiled.

'Cheer up, Nurse Scott!' she exclaimed. 'You'll have escaped from this ward next week. All the nurses tell me that surgery is much more exciting!'

'I shall miss Belton, Sister. I've really enjoyed working here.'

Sister looked suddenly serious. 'Well, we've enjoyed having you. You've fitted in well, and worked hard. I know a lot of people said that an ex-model wouldn't stick it for more than a week, but you've proved them wrong.' She hesitated for a moment. 'Look, I think you've got the makings of a really excellent nurse, and if you should ever decide that medical nursing is your preference—well, I'd be pleased to have you Staff here on Belton.'

'Why, thank . . . thank you very much, Sister,' stammered Claire. She felt extremely honoured—Sister Thompson was a woman she really admired, and if she thought she could do it . . . well, she would show all the sceptics.

At the end of report Sister turned to her. 'Derek Ronaldson is still with us, I'm afraid. They've had a bit of trouble stabilising his diabetes, and he hasn't exactly been co-operative. Perhaps you could have a word with him later, Nurse Scott—he seems to like you.'

Claire nodded and, putting her small notebook in her pocket, she followed Anna Hunter out to do the drug round.

It was the patients' tea-time by the time she found a moment to talk to Derry. As she approached his bed, she noticed that he was looking glumly at a small plain biscuit on his tray.

'Cheer up,' she chided. 'It might never happen!'

He glowered at her. 'It already has,' he remarked gloomily. 'Anyway, look who's talking! I thought you might trip up today, you've had such a long face. What's the matter with you? Boyfriend troubles?'

Claire blushed. Derry had a sharp eye. She wondered who else had noticed.

'It's you I've come to talk about,' she rejoined, quickly changing the subject. 'Why are you glaring at that poor defenceless biscuit?'

He turned on her. 'Have you seen what the others are eating?'

She looked round. It was Mr Perkins' birthday, and his wife had brought in a huge chocolate gateau and was handing plates of it out to all the patients.

'Oh, Derry,' she said, and sat on the edge of his bed, 'it's only a piece of cake! When you really get to grips with your condition, you'll be able to make your own cakes, or eat chocolate occasionally. There are all types of sugar substitutes on the market these days. Honestly, Derry,' her voice was ardent, 'you can buy sugarless drinks at any small shop or pub in the whole country. Imagine how difficult things were for diabetes sufferers ten years ago. You've been diagnosed while you're still very young, so you'll be able to make any changes to your lifestyle before you're really set in your ways. But there shouldn't be that many changes—you can lead as normal a life as *you* want to.'

He was silent for a minute, then gave her his cheeky grin. 'OK, Nurse,' he said resignedly. 'You can get down off your soapbox now. You've browbeaten me into submission! You can even have my share of the cake, if you like!'

Claire laughed and at the back of her mind felt a wave of relief that her sense of humour hadn't completely disappeared.

He began to tell her something of his way of life. He was a roadie with a struggling rock band. They travelled in an old van up and down the country, and meals tended to be snatched plates of chips in motorway cafés or sandwiches eaten on the run.

'There's absolutely no routine about the job,' he told her. 'No areas of constancy at all. And some forward planning is necessary if you're a diabetic—well, that's what Dr Hayward told me before he left.'

Claire started at the mention of Luke's name. 'What do your parents say?' she asked.

He shrugged. 'They've always been very supportive, but they wish I'd go to university. I got good grades at "A" level and I was hoping to read anthropology.'

She patted the back of his hand. 'Why don't you think about doing that? You could always go back to being with a band afterwards. You'd have a great time at college—and you'd have the support of your tutor, or even the university doctor, to help you with your diabetes.'

She looked at the clock and gave a yelp of horror. 'Listen, Derry, I must go. Think about it anyway, and I'll come and talk to you later, if you like.'

He gripped her hand. 'Claire, you're an angel!'

She faced him indignantly. 'How did you know my name?'

He shook his long blond hair from out of his face and winked. 'I overheard one of the doctors.'

As she hurried off to answer a bell, she wondered who that might have been. Bill Dixon, probably.

Four-thirty. Five hours until she was off duty. Claire sighed. An empty flat and an empty bed awaited her.

As long as she was busy, she was fine. Work became her refuge, there was never time to miss Luke, except in very fleeting moments, let alone moon about him.

It was the evenings which seemed interminably long, when she tried not to hang around the telephone. He had rung twice that first week, but it was frustrating not being able to see him and touch him. And she wasn't due to see him until the end of the month. The pain of missing him was almost physical.

She had tried imagining the perfect scenario—of Luke ringing to tell her that he loved her, that he couldn't live without her and would she go up to Scotland to be with him?

But was that really the answer? What would she do up there while her busy doctor worked every hour that God sent? He had already told her on the phone that Professor Hempstock was brilliant, but a fairly intolerant slave-driver.

Besides, she owed it to herself to complete her training. You couldn't just start something like nursing and then give it up without a very good reason. It would let everyone down.

Almost overnight, summer became autumn. The leaves began to change from green to orange and gold, and strong winds tugged relentlessly at them, so that some swirled in flurries, like darkened snowflakes.

Claire left Belton Ward and started on Bluebell, the general female surgical ward. She said a sad farewell to Sister Thompson and the other girls. Staff Lee was now Staff Nurse Stafford, married to the infamous Nigel and living in married bliss in Kentish Town.

Derek Ronaldson had left the ward and had given her a huge box of chocolates. 'I shan't be able to eat these,' he had joked. He told her that he had decided to go to university next autumn, and was planning to work on a farm in Somerset during the interim year.

'Some friends of my parents,' he had explained. 'She's a wonderful cook, and there's a daughter there who's nearly as gorgeous as you, seeing as how you're spoken for.'

'How on earth do you know I'm spoken for?' Claire had asked in astonishment.

He had winked. 'It's written in your eyes, I can tell.'

Bluebell Ward was like stepping on to another planet. For a start, the whole routine was entirely different from the medical ward and there was a rapid turnover of patients, which made it very confusing for Claire at first, as there never seemed to be a face she could recognise.

Mary's warning about Sister Fulton had not been exaggerated. She was an attractive woman of about thirty with thick shiny hair the colour of a ginger biscuit. But her brown eyes could look mean and her small, neat mouth rarely smiled. Except, of course, when Mr Denham the Surgical Registrar was about. Then she emerged from her cocoon of an office and began to scurry around the ward, stripping beds, offering drinks, checking intravenous infusions and fluid charts. It was the only time that Claire ever saw her out on the ward, unlike Sister Thompson, who would always roll up her sleeves and join in.

And at the end of his ward round, she would sidle up to Mr Denham and purse her cyclamen-painted lips and say: 'Kettle's on, and I'm ready when you are, Mark.'

Just what Mark thought about all this, no one knew, but he used to trot behind her into the office where they would drink Earl Grey tea from china cups, and eat the rich German coffee cake which Sister always provided.

Or so Claire was told by another first-year who was a set above her. Viola Kennett was an irrepressible gossip.

'I'm Sister's favourite,' she confided to Claire. 'But only because I'm as plain as a pikestaff!'

It was true. Viola's appearance did not match her elegant name—she was a broadly built, very muscular girl with a tight mass of light brown curls which she claimed never grew more than two inches in length.

'I should be seen and not heard on this ward, if I

were you,' she advised Claire, wrinkling her wide freckled face comically. 'That way Sister won't be able to pick on you.'

Claire tried to keep her head down. There was so much that was new to her, so much to learn. All patients who were going down to theatre for their operation had to be starved from the previous midnight. Any body hair over the operation site had to be shaved off, and the site itself marked by the surgeon, in indelible ink. This was to guard against the wrong limb or organ being operated on. Any jewellery had to be removed and locked away, except for wedding rings which were allowed to be taped to the finger. Nail varnish, which could disguise the ominous blueness of the fingertips, known as cyanosis, had to be cleaned off. False teeth were taken out and the patient dressed in a thin white hospital gown and a paper cap to await an injection of opiate to sedate and calm, coupled with a drug to prevent sickness.

All morning long, porters arrived with narrow trolleys and patients were dispatched to theatre with their notes and X-rays, and the nurse accompanying them would often escort another patient back to the ward.

Post-operatively, the patient needed frequent and regular observation. Pulse and blood pressure were checked every fifteen minutes to begin with, and these periods were gradually lengthened to every half-hour and then every hour, provided that the patient's condition gave no cause for concern.

Claire quickly learnt to give the groggy patients

pink mouthwash to alleviate the dryness in their mouths, caused by starving and the various anaesthetic drugs. As they became less groggy, she would offer them tiny sips of iced water.

To her dismay, she discovered that Alex Morris-Clarke was the newly qualified house surgeon on Bluebell. She had been on the ward for three days and he had said nothing to her, but had given her the occasional withering look.

On her fourth day, she had been hurrying back from lunch and they had almost collided by the lift outside the ward.

'Well, well, well,' he had drawled lazily, his lips curving back in what was almost a snarl. 'It's the hospital's living symbol of female subordination!'

Claire looked steadily back at him, at his tall elegantly-clad figure, wearing the spotty bow tie which he always affected. She didn't like the expression in his eyes at all. How could she have ever thought that he was amusing?

'Excuse me,' she said, trying to brush past him, but he grabbed her by the shoulder.

'How touching,' he snarled softly, 'that you should have aroused such stirring feelings of chivalry from the highly respected Dr Hayward! Tell me,' his mocking face moved close to hers, 'did he send you home with a slap on the hand, or did he extract some suitable reward for rescuing a damsel in distress?'

She felt uneasy, and intimidated, but she would not let him know that. 'Oh, shut up, Alex,' she answered crossly. 'And be your age. The subject's not for discussion, and I'd appreciate it if you'd let me get back to work now.'

She pushed past him and with a thumping heart, went to hang her cloak up.

She was busy all afternoon, and before she realised it, saw that the ward clock read four forty-five. She should have been off duty fifteen minutes ago.

Tentatively, she made her way to Sister's office and tapped lightly on the door. A low voice called 'Come in' and Claire stepped inside, to find Alex sitting on Sister's desk, his long legs crossed, and a tea-cup by his side.

'Yes—what is it, Nurse?' demanded Sister shortly.

'Please, may I go off duty now, Sister? I'm on an early.'

The brown eyes surveyed her as though she had been an insect on the carpet. 'No, you may not go off duty now. You will go off when I tell you, and not a moment before. In my student days we had the good manners to wait until the senior nurse dismissed us. We were not the clockwatchers you girls today seem to be. Now please go back on to the ward until I give you permission to leave.'

Claire couldn't miss Alex's snigger as he raised the tea-cup to his lips.

She mechanically went round the ward, busying herself with the charts. She helped another nurse sit a patient up.

'Why aren't you off duty?' the nurse hissed at Claire, and Claire shrugged, not daring to speak in case she made a fool of herself and started blubbering.

Sister eventually gave her permission to leave at five-fifteen, an expression of distaste on her face as she did so. 'And don't be late in the morning,' she told her unnecessarily. Claire had not been late for any duty once.

Claire made her way down the main corridor, with a dull throbbing ache across her forehead. She bit her lip and mentally told herself to pull herself together. She felt utterly miserable.

Luke had only been gone ten days, but it might as well have been ten years—she felt so lonely. And now she was working on an alien ward with a hostile Ward Sister and a resentful, carping Morris-Clarke. Luke wasn't due down to see her until the end of the month—how on earth was she going to survive?

On the off-chance, she called into Mary's room in the Nurses' Home, but there was no reply. A quietly spoken Welsh girl came out of the adjoining room and asked, 'Are you looking for Mary Wells?'

Claire nodded bleakly.

'Oh, she's gone to live with her boyfriend.' There was the wide smile of delight at being able to pass on an exciting piece of news. 'Didn't you know?'

Claire shook her head. She walked across the quadrangle to where she kept her bicycle. The wind was biting and she pulled her gabardine closer. More leaves had fallen and lay in small crunchy piles in shades of crimson and russet and gold outside the bike shed.

When she got back to the flat, she changed out of her uniform into jeans and a sweater. She would try ringing Mary at Simon's. She held the receiver to her ear.

There were three and a half loud rings and then a click and a whirr, and a recorded message began. It was Simon's voice. 'Hi,' it said. 'This is Simon and Mary's phone. We're sorry wc're not here to take your message, but if you leave your name and number we'll get back to you as soon as we can. Please speak after the bleep.'

Claire listened to the mechanical tone, and stared blankly at the receiver, then replaced it. She couldn't believe it—Simon was actually acknowledging Mary's presence on his answering machine—he must be really serious. She felt pleased for her friend.

And a little jealous too, aren't you? nagged a small voice in her head. But she wasn't jealous of Mary, just resentful of a fate which should have dragged Luke from her life so soon.

She hadn't told anyone about her relationship with him, not Mary, and certainly not her mother. Her mother would be appalled if she knew that they had been sleeping together; she had always impressed on Claire that sex should only come after marriage.

She felt as though she would be tempting an already fickle fate if she announced to all and sundry that she was having an affair with the gorgeous Dr Hayward. Besides, it seemed so long since he had held her in his arms that she could hardly believe it herself.

At that moment the phone began to ring noisily and she jumped.

'Hello?' she said softly, then her heart leapt as she heard his deep voice.

'Hello, darling—it's me.'

'Luke!' she cried excitedly. 'I was just thinking about you—how are you?'

'I'm fine, sweetheart. Now listen, I think I may be able to get down next weekend.'

'But I'm working!' she wailed.

'I don't care. I want to see you. I miss you.'

Tears slid down Claire's face. 'I miss you too.' She lay on the sofa, the receiver to her ear, and listened while he told her he would arrive on Saturday week.

'But you were supposed to be coming down the following weekend, anyway,' she pointed out.

She could tell he was smiling. 'Then you'll just have to put up with me for two weeks running!'

Claire felt as though she had been given the most wonderful present in the world. Even Sister Fulton was unable to dampen her enthusiasm, while she found Alex's occasional nasty asides positively pathetic.

She began to plan for Luke's homecoming as though he had been away at sea for years. When she wasn't studying or working, she was methodically cleaning every inch of the flat or poring over cookery books to find the most perfect meal to concoct for him.

She spent over an hour talking to the wine merchant before finally deciding to blow the expense and drink a fruity pink champagne with the meal.

The ward was busy that week, and one patient had a cardiac arrest following routine surgery and almost died.

Claire was on an early on Saturday and a late on

Sunday, but she had the Friday off. She bought armfuls of flowers, stately great balls of chrysanthemums in autumnal yellows and golds. She opened windows and the newly cleaned curtains fluttered in the September breeze.

The flat smelt of polish and flowers and a lemon and raisin cake which she'd spent the afternoon baking. She listened to the Wagnerian opera Luke had played in his car that night. It didn't suit her happy mood, but it was something of him. She longed for him.

Just after six, the phone rang, and as she picked it up she heard the faint pip which told her it was long-distance.

'Hello?' she said.

There was a pause, then she heard Luke's voice, and before he had completed one word, she knew what he was going to say, that something had come up, that he would not be coming.

'Hello, sweetheart, I've got some bad news, I'm afraid. Professor Hempstock has invited me to supper at his house. He wants me to meet his wife. I'm so sorry, sweetheart, but it can't be helped—I really ought to go. And darling, I'll still be able to come next weekend—and you'll be off then. Claire? Are you still there?'

'Yes, I'm still here. Don't worry, we'll still have next weekend.'

They spoke for a few minutes, but afterwards Claire couldn't remember what they had said. She knew she was being unreasonable, but she felt angry and upset. Her hopes had been raised and then dashed. And why couldn't Luke have told his Professor that he had a prior engagement?

Because his work came first—she knew that. He was having a very pleasant affair, but his career was more important, and you didn't pass up supper with your boss just because you had some eager young nurse waiting to cook you supper and leap into bed with you.

Mechanically she began to tip the orange sorbet which she had half prepared into the waste-disposal unit.

She hated it—the snatched moments, the impersonal telephone calls and the uncertainty of it all. She wondered how long they would be able to carry on like this.

Luke replaced the receiver with a sigh. Dusk was beginning to fall on the city, shadows deepening and blotting out buildings until soon it resembled any other city by night.

He liked Glasgow. He had never been there before his interview and had known little about it, save for the running jokes about it being a giant slum. But it wasn't. The South's prejudice had done it an injustice—he found its tall, dark buildings imposing, and the atmosphere unbelievably lively. And he had been unprepared for the disarming friendliness of the Glaswegians themselves.

His medical colleagues had gone out of their way to welcome him, and it seemed that everyone, from the elderly woman who cleaned his flat, to the staff in the canteen, was open and funny and charming.

He should have been happy. The job was hard and demanding. His boss was a fastidious tyrant, but one who was conducting some of the finest research in Europe. His work into Crohn's disease was not merely the esoteric writing of a brilliant intellect, designed to impress and intimidate his peers. No, if Professor Hempstock's research could show a definite cause of the disease, then a cure was in sight, and thousands of sufferers world-wide could be helped. Luke felt proud and honoured to be a member of the team, and it made him realise that he had started to get into a rut at St Anthony's.

So what was the problem? He sighed again. It was Claire. He shouldn't have rung up like that on the spur of the moment to say he would see her, and then let her down. She had sounded upset, and it was not surprising. He *did* miss her, more than he could ever have believed possible.

She had burrowed her way into his heart, and it was making him miserable. He didn't want things to be this way—so that he found it difficult to concentrate on his work. Affairs of the heart always complicated things—why else had he spent all these years carefully avoiding any commitment?

He wanted to be a consultant and he wanted to be the best. And to be the best you had to have a driving force, a single-mindedness which could easily be called selfishness. To get to the top he did not need a young girl tantalising him at every minute of the day, when he should be studying.

He'd seen marriages made in haste all the way through his career, and he had seen the casualties.

Couples parted geographically because of jobs. The long hours and the loneliness. People thrown together at parties—too much to drink. And then what? Infidelity, recrimination and heartbreak.

And what of Claire? He was not even offering her marriage. How could he ask her to marry him when they had only known each other properly—he smiled wryly at his use of the word—for inside the month?

He'd wanted to be a friend to her, and he'd failed. He had set her on the path to nursing and she was proving to be a good nurse. Sister Thompson had told him that she thought Claire was a born nurse.

And he had spoilt it all. He hadn't really tried at all to offer any resistance to her charms. She had almost three years' training still ahead of her, and he was subjecting her to these brief moments of heady passion.

Heady passion because it was rationed? Their lives ruled by the clock. Was this fair to Claire? Or to him?

His head was spinning, but he felt a familiar pulse beating steadily, hypnotically. Just thinking about it did nothing. He still wanted her. Perhaps he should have a serious talk with her next weekend.

CHAPTER THIRTEEN

BUT by next morning, things appeared far less gloomy than they had the previous evening, and Claire felt cross with herself for allowing herself to sink into despondency.

She was seeing Luke next weekend, and the anticipation would make the wait worth while. She *must* stop moaning, or she wouldn't be much of a companion!

She still had all the food which she had bought for his visit. She would phone Mary and Simon up at coffee-time and invite them over for supper.

At ten, when Claire telephoned, Simon said they would love to come. 'What are you working?' he asked sleepily.

'I'm on half-day—off at midday.'

'Great!' said Simon. 'I've just had an idea. We'll be round at one o'clock and take you for a drink. Is that OK?'

'Yes, that's fine,' agreed Claire, wondering what he was up to.

She made beds with Viola, did two bed-baths and then after coffee was sent to clean out the sluice.

'And try to do something with your hair, will you, Scott?' said Sister Fulton irritably. 'It looks as though you've been dragged through a hedge backwards!'

This was patently not true. The copper curls were mostly hidden beneath Claire's cap. Perhaps Sister would like her to shave her head, thought Claire disrespectfully, as she attacked the test-tubes with a wire cleaner.

Surprisingly enough, Sister let her off duty punctually, then she spotted the reason why. Sister Fulton disappeared through the swing doors with Mark Denham, shouting to the third-year who was left in charge, 'I'm off to lunch now!'

Outside, a brilliant golden sun shone through the branches, making patterns like a honeycomb on the path. Wisps of white clouds blew past like puffs of smoke, and as Claire back-pedalled down Haverstock Hill, she felt a rush of freedom and exhilaration.

She arrived home and had just changed into blue cords and an ice-cream pink sweater when Simon and Mary arrived, smiling happily and bearing two bottles of wine, a tub of coffee and walnut ice-cream and a huge spray of orange carnations which they presented with a flourish.

Claire raised her eyebrows.

'It's Simon—he's feeling generous. I don't know what's got into him today,' giggled Mary, as she pulled off her jacket. Claire thought she had never seen her look so radiant, the picture of glowing health and youth as she stood next to Simon.

He winked at Claire. 'It's Mary's birthday tomorrow, did you know?' and she shook her head, feeling slightly guilty that her own preoccupations seemed to have excluded the rest of the world.

'Pop this wine in the fridge, will you, my angel?'

He thrust a bottle into Mary's hand and she disappeared into the kitchen.

'Make an excuse to go out and buy beer and say you need me to carry it,' he hissed at Claire.

When Mary returned, Claire went though the pantomime of looking in the fridge for a beer for Simon and suggested she go out and buy some.

'I'll help you carry it,' said Simon hastily.

'Why don't we all go?' asked Mary in a puzzled voice.

'To be honest, I want Claire to help me choose an appallingly tasteless birthday card for you,' said Simon. 'So you just sit here and read a magazine, or write a letter, or something.'

'Oh, all right,' laughed Mary. 'You win.'

Claire and Simon left, banging the door behind them, and Mary settled down on the sofa, leafing through a glossy magazine. It was an old one, and one in which Claire had featured. She peered with interest at a white-faced, gaunt-looking Claire, the dark red brick and gold trim of the Albert Hall in the background. She noticed that the photos were accredited to Simon Saunders.

The minutes ticked by, and they were still not back. An hour became two hours and she was beginning to get worried when the telephone burst into a shrill ringing beside her, making her jump.

'Hello,' she said tentatively, then read the number off.

'Is Claire there, please?' asked a male voice.

'No, I'm sorry. She's out—she's gone out with Simon and they were supposed to have been back by now. I don't know where they've got to. Can I leave a message?'

There was a long pause. 'No, that's all right. No message.'

'Who shall I say . . .?' began Mary, then stopped. The man had hung up.

Then she heard running footsteps and a key in the lock and there stood Claire and Simon, grinning all over their faces.

'There you are!' she said accusingly. 'Where have you been?'

Luke sat quietly for a moment, his heart beating very fast. He kept thinking how ironic it was—he had been worried about Claire leading a dull, monastic life, waiting around for him, and now it seemed that she was certainly not sitting at home moping. He felt as though someone was turning a knife in his guts at the thought of her with someone else. Who the hell was Simon anyway?

Then he remembered—it was the glamour boy he'd first seen her with, that night in the restaurant. He didn't know that they were close friends. But then what did he know about her life in general? Or she his? She had never introduced him to any of her friends. They had done very little else in three weeks, other than to chase each other around the bedroom.

She was a sweet, beautiful girl. If circumstances had been different, then there might have been a future for them, but it was not fair to either of them to expect that such a protracted courtship should endure.

Claire deserved someone younger, someone who

could give her all the attention and love she surely warranted, and she would never find him while he was around.

With a hand that felt almost as heavy as his heart, Luke picked up his pen and began to write.

There were shrieks and yells of excitement as Simon pulled the ring out of the small box and put it on Mary's finger.

Claire discreetly left the room for champagne as they embraced. She carried it back through with three glasses, thinking how she had planned to drink it with Luke that night, and instead she was celebrating Simon and Mary's engagement.

As she entered the room they turned. Mary was laughing and looking at her finger and Simon was smiling bashfully. He took the bottle from Claire and the cork flew out with a mighty pop.

They chinked glasses. Claire picked up Mary's hand and examined it closely. 'I'm so happy for you both. It's a beautiful ring, Mary.'

'Isn't it?' asked Mary in delight before turning to look up at Simon. 'I never thought I'd own an emerald—I really didn't!'

'I just wanted someone to tell me I was buying the right kind of thing,' he explained, and grinned like a schoolboy before sipping some wine. 'But I wanted it to be a surprise, that's why I asked Claire to help me.' He turned to Claire and his eyes were serious. 'You know, I owe a lot to you, Claire. If you hadn't decided to become a nurse, then I'd never have met Mary —and she's made me happier than I've ever been.

I think we ought to drink a toast to Claire.' He paused for a moment. 'To Claire.'

'To Claire,' echoed Mary, and they all chinked glasses again. And in all the excitement, Mary quite forgot to tell Claire that she'd had a phone call.

CHAPTER FOURTEEN

THE LETTER arrived by second post on Tuesday and came just as Claire was leaving the flat to start a late duty.

She looked at the white envelope, the distinctive spidery handwriting in black ink—and the foreboding which had been at the back of her mind for almost a month crept stealthily out. She ripped open the envelope and with a trembling hand pulled out the single sheet of paper. It was as she had thought. The words on the paper swam. She tried to read them and failed, then tried again. It read:

> My dear Claire,
>
> This is a very difficult letter for me to write, and I hope you will forgive me for not having the courage to say this to you personally.
>
> I think it probably best if we don't see each other, at least for the time being. I feel, and I imagine that you do too, very strongly about you, more strongly than I've felt about anyone for a long time, perhaps ever. But I'm also aware that the distance between us, with you tied to St Anthony's for three years, and me working at the other end of the country, is putting an incredible strain on us both.

I don't feel it's fair to expect you to live a cloistered life around my infrequent visits, while at the same time, I know I couldn't bear to think of you seeing anyone else, however casually.

I feel you're very young, and that these are some of the best years of your life, and that you should be going out and enjoying yourself, and having fun. I am, after all, a staid man—teetering on the brink of middle age!

The reason that I'm writing this, instead of telling you, is that I fear my resolve would weaken were I to see you.

I hope that one day you might be able to thank me for writing this letter, and also that one day you might find it in your heart to think of me as your friend.

Yours ever,
Luke.

Claire tried to take it in, but the enormity of it was beyond her. And all the time T.S. Eliot's lines kept repeating inside her head, like some ancient incantation: 'This is the way the world ends, Not with a bang but with a whimper.'

She wished she could crawl into a corner and hide, like some wounded animal, but she couldn't. She stared at her face in the hall mirror, astounded that externally it should look the same, that there was not one hint of the pain she felt inside.

Except perhaps that the eyes looked empty, perhaps the torment could be glimpsed there. She must get going, she mustn't be late for work.

Somehow she unlocked her pushbike. She began to cycle, pushing her way up Haverstock Hill. The wind felt icy, her legs were leaden. Her fingers felt almost too numb to grip the rubber of the handlebars.

And then it hit her. However carefully Luke had couched it, whatever kind and caring words he used—it was over. He would never again hold her in his arms, to kiss and comfort her. The voyage was over, it was finished.

A great hollow sob erupted from her, and she had no power to stop it, and the tears which had lain dormant sprouted from her eyes so that they blinded her.

She vaguely heard a frenzied blaring of someone's car horn. And all the driver of the van saw, all he remembered, was her tiny face, dead white and curiously frozen. Her body seemed to spring off the bike until it lay, awkward, like a puppet in the road.

As he bent down over her, he was struck by the brightness of her hair, brighter even than the blood that trickled down her cheek and dried there, like a curl.

CHAPTER FIFTEEN

THE AMBULANCE took Claire straight to St Anthony's. The two crewmen lifted her carefully on to a stretcher while the van driver stood there, with fear in his eyes. 'She just came out of nowhere—honestly!' he cried wildly. 'Is she—is she going to be all right?'

'We shan't know yet,' answered one of them as he closed the back doors. They switched the siren on and roared off towards the hospital.

In Casualty, the casualty officer and the senior Sister stood waiting to receive them, their faces serious. Their emergency red telephone had rung a few minutes earlier, to tell them that one of their nurses had been knocked off her bike by a car. The department seemed quieter than usual. They did not like to see one of their own injured.

Claire was taken directly to the resuscitation cubicle, where a worried-looking casualty officer bent over her to start examining her. She began to moan.

'She's coming round, Sister!'

The milky white swathes in front of her eyes began to disappear and Claire found herself looking at an anxious young doctor. She tried to sit up, but his firm hand restrained her.

'You're not going anywhere, Claire,' he told her quietly. 'You've had a nasty knock on the head. Can you remember what happened?'

She shook her head and managed a glimmer of a smile, and then it all came back to her, and the pain of it eclipsed even the throbbing on the right side of her head, which had started to ache alarmingly. She wished she could just go to sleep and wake up to find that the whole episode had been an awful nightmare, that Luke had never written the letter, better even that she had never met him.

'You'll have to be admitted, you know,' the doctor was saying as he shone a torch into both her eyes. 'Hmm. Both pupils reacting well—good girl!'

'I feel fine,' she murmured, as he tapped her knees and elbows with his patella hammer. 'Must I be admitted, Sister?'

Sister was filling in a form. 'Yes, of course you must, m'dear. You know that really, don't you?'

Claire nodded. She didn't feel *that* bad. Apart from the headache she just felt a bit sleepy. The casualty officer was telling her how lucky she was. She wished he would go away—she didn't feel very lucky today.

She gave Sister her name and address, age, religion and the name of her general practitioner. She gave her mother as next of kin.

'But she's on holiday in America at the moment,' she explained. 'Sister, my friend is working in Casualty—may I be allowed to see her before I go to the ward?'

Sister frowned slightly, but she felt sorry for this pretty young nurse with the sad eyes.

'Very well—but only for a couple of minutes, mind! What's her name?'

Claire gave her Mary's name, and a few minutes later an ashen-faced Mary appeared.

'Claire!' she exclaimed, and took Claire's hand in hers. 'What on earth has happened?'

Claire looked at Sister beseechingly. 'Please may I just have one minute to speak privately with Nurse Wells?'

Sister looked from one to the other, then nodded. 'I'll be back in two minutes, but don't tire her out. Come on, Doctor.'

As soon as they had left, Claire's lip began to buckle and tears crept down her cheeks.

Mary looked at her in horror—this wasn't the Claire she knew. 'Don't cry, Claire. You're going to be all right. Don't cry.'

Claire shook her head mutely. When she spoke her voice was shaking. 'I'm so miserable, Mary. Do you remember Luke Hayward? I introduced him to you once in the canteen?'

Mary nodded. 'How could I forget—the hunk who lent you the textbook, or something. What about him?'

Claire could hardly speak. 'I should have told you. We—we went out for a bit, and I thought it was serious. Then he had to go to Glasgow—he's got a new job up there.' Her eyes were pleading. 'I mean, I knew that, Mary, but I still thought . . .' She gulped, trying to swallow back the tears.

'Anyway, today I received a letter from him. He—he thinks it best if we don't see each other. I was cycling to work, I couldn't have been concentrating. I was crying—it was my fault. Oh, Mary, I love him so much!'

She began to sob, one hand covering her eyes, brushing fronds of matted hair away.

Mary's lips tightened. 'The bastard!' she muttered, and her grey eyes darkened with anger. 'Claire, listen. You mustn't cry—you mustn't. He's not worth your tears, and you've got to concentrate on getting better.' She gripped her friend's hand tightly. 'Besides, I've got some news that will cheer you up. Guess which ward you're being admitted to?'

Claire shrugged weakly.

'Bluebell!'

In spite of everything, Claire managed a smile. 'Not the dreaded Sister Fulton?' she whispered.

Casualty Sister reappeared and looked at Mary approvingly. 'Good—I can see you've managed to cheer her up. I'd let you accompany her to the ward, but I really ought to send someone who's qualified. You can visit her later.'

'I'll come and see you when I'm off duty,' hissed Mary. 'But don't forget what I said. It's not worth crying about.'

Claire nodded and watched her friend leave. As she was being transferred to a trolley, she could hear Sister saying, 'Make sure she's on fifteen-minute neurological observation for the next four hours at least.'

Then she was being pushed along the main corridor, past curious faces, up in the lift and on to Bluebell. Sister Fulton came straight up to her. To Claire's surprise, there was a look of genuine concern on the older woman's face.

'I'm so sorry you've had an accident, Claire. We'll keep an eye on you here, let's hope just overnight. First cubicle, opposite the office, please,' she told the porter.

They lifted her on to the bed. Claire tried to clear the fuzziness out of her head. She held her arm out to have her blood pressure taken. Things were beginning to take on a dreamlike quality. She could see Sister's mouth opening and closing, but no words were coming out. And they were shining that stupid torch in her eyes *again*.

'I don't want any more cotton wool in my ears!' she shouted at them. And now they were turning all the lights out, it was getting darker and darker.

Just before she entered the tunnel she saw Sister's startled face, and the frightened face of the Casualty staff nurse, and then the silence became a roar in her ears, and everything went black.

The curious thing was that Luke had derived no pleasure or satisfaction in knowing that he had regained his freedom. He tried to tell himself how much better off Claire would be without him, but his justifications sounded false and hypocritical.

He had walked to the postbox on Saturday evening, down Bayres Road and into Sauchiehall Street—the strange names which were gradually becoming familiar. He watched the envelope disappear with a finality that suggested that a chapter of his life was over.

After he had posted it he walked up to Park Circus, where the whole city lay spread in front of him, like a tablecloth.

That evening he had been persuaded to go to a party in the doctors' mess, where a stunning-looking staff nurse had spent the evening smiling up at him and clinging to his arm, but he had remained immune. He had seen her look of surprise when he had abruptly announced that he was leaving.

He had lain awake for hours, unable to rid himself of Claire's memory. The best thing that had ever happened to him had been thrown on to the sacrificial fire of his precious career.

Just what was it he wanted—a career? At what cost? His happiness? Was his job going to monopolise his life and exclude any family he might one day have? Wasn't that what his father had done, hadn't that been part of the problem? Was he simply going to repeat the mistakes of his parents—was that why he was so frightened of committing himself?

But destiny wasn't a ready-made entity that dropped into your lap at birth—it was as malleable as a piece of damp clay, he could mould it to whatever form he desired.

There had been no one to touch his heart in quite the way that Claire had, not ever. And he had felt out of his depth. He had thrown her most precious gift of love back in her face. What an emotional lightweight he was! And just what was he going to do about it?

On Sunday he was unable to do any work on his research, and by Tuesday he could think of nothing else. So much for being able to concentrate on his work again—this was far worse.

He couldn't face any lunch and instead went to his

room, where he sat at his desk, wondering if he went to see Claire—to ask her to forgive him for his doubts and stupidity—whether she would slam the door in his face. He wouldn't blame her.

But already, just the thought of making it all right between them again was setting his heart racing. He would spend the rest of his life making it up to her.

And at precisely that moment, the harsh jangling of the phone broke into his thoughts and shattered them.

CHAPTER SIXTEEN

IT WAS a journey Luke was never to forget. In a blur, as though he was observing someone else, he remembered telling his Professor that his fiancée had been involved in a bad accident. He had said 'fiancée' desperately—afraid that his boss would not let him go. Yet even as he said it he knew that he was prepared to go anyway, even if it meant that he had no job to come back to.

But the older man had seen such a terrifying look of grief on the face of his Senior Registrar that he had arranged for someone to drive him to the airport.

'May God go with you,' he had said gruffly.

Luke arrived at the airport with nothing save his cheque-book and wallet, and it was Professor Hempstock's secretary who guided him through various checkpoints until he found himself buckled into a window seat, staring blankly as the plane gathered height and the countryside became a toytown.

The angry, bitter words of the girl came back to him. 'I'm Claire's friend Mary. There's been a bad accident—Claire's been hit by a van. She's on the neuro-surgical ward. They don't know if she's going to make it.'

She had to make it. Please! Luke pleaded silently,

clenching his fists until the nails scratched his palms.

'There's no next of kin here,' she had gone on. 'She seems to think a lot of you—though God knows why. Could you . . .' she had broken down then and he had heard uncontrolled sobbing at the other end of the line. 'Please come! Please come and tell her you love her—tell her any lies you like, but help make her better.'

He had felt calm then. 'I'll come,' he said briefly. 'And I'll tell her all those things, and more. But they won't be lies—not one word of them.'

Afterwards he was able to recollect little of the journey, which in itself was odd, since so many images printed themselves clearly on his mind while the plane was in motion.

He found himself looking at all the women on the flight, wondering what it was about fate that should have selected Claire—sweet, innocent Claire—to be lying stricken in a hospital bed, awaiting surgery whose outcome was doubtful.

He tried not to stare at the stewardesses, with their neat hairstyles and their carefully painted-on smiles. Claire had once shown him her portfolio, and even in her modelling days, hers had never been a contrived kind of beauty. She had always had an element of the wild and the carefree about her.

He remembered as though it were yesterday that first time he had seen her sitting in the restaurant, as restless as a caged cat, the boredom and the disillusionment naked in her eyes.

So many things about her. The pictures came crowding back rapidly, each one pushing the other out of his memory, vying for position there.

The time when he had seen her walking down the ward, her back so straight and proud. Or the time when they had stood by the river-bank that last evening, when he should have told her he loved her, but hadn't. The first time they had made love, and he had dried her tears.

The joy she had brought him. Tender, uncomplicated joy. The memories came swiftly—they had no chronology.

How could he have been so commonplace, so prosaic as to imagine that the time they had spent together was too short for words of commitment? To his tortured mind now, it seemed as though they had spent at least one lifetime together. And there might never be time to tell her this.

He sat, completely unaware of the flirtatious glances directed at him by the stewardess, as the plane came in to land at Heathrow.

He jumped into a black cab at the taxi rank, and the toothless Cockney in the driver's seat looked taken aback when Luke named his destination.

'It'll cost yer, guv'nor,' he said, a questioning look on his face.

'I don't care,' said Luke gruffly. 'Just get there as quickly as you can.'

'Will do.' The cab roared off. 'Doctor, are you?'

'Yes, that's right.' Luke answered automatically.

The driver nodded, a pleased expression on his face. 'I can always tell.'

How he did it without being stopped by the police, Luke never knew, but in under an hour they were pulling up outside the main gates of St Anthony's.

As he ran towards the lift, ignoring the fundamental hospital teaching of only running in cases of fire or haemorrhage, he was aware only of feeling helpless. This must be how patients' relatives feel, he thought as the lift travelled up towards the neuro-surgical ward—unable to do anything other than watch, and wait.

He walked into Sister's office, to see the grave face of Miles Channon standing looking at X-rays in front of the light box.

He stepped forward before he could stop himself and asked, 'Are they Claire's?'

The tall, thin neuro-surgeon nodded, and stepped back, knowing when to expect the inevitable.

Luke was expecting the worst, but when it came it was like ice-water hitting him in the face. He could see the skull fracture lying over the artery. It could only mean . . .

His eyes met Miles's. 'Is it——?' The voice could barely be heard.

Miles Channon cleared his throat. 'I'm afraid so, dear chap. She has an extra-dural haemorrhage. We'll be operating within the hour.'

Luke's face was grey and he felt Sister's hands on his arm, trying to guide him to a chair, but he pushed them away roughly.

'What happened? What the hell happened?' His voice sounded peculiar, even to himself.

'She was knocked off her bicycle by a van, sustained a blow to the skull and lost consciousness for a short time. She came round in Casualty and her observations were fine.

'We transferred her to a surgical ward, Neurosurgery having, as you know, several beds closed, where her condition gave cause for concern.' Miles Channon stood reciting the facts. 'Her left pupil became larger, and did not react to light. Her blood pressure increased to 170/100 and her pulse rate dropped to fifty-six. She lost consciousness. She was transferred here and scanned, and this has confirmed our fears, namely that she has an extra-dural haemorrhage, requiring Burr holes.'

For a moment Luke stood there staring at his colleague, his breathing sounding harsh and laboured.

'So what does that mean?' he asked desperately. 'What are her chances?'

Miles Channon's eyebrows shot up, and he looked mildly surprised. 'Well, you know that, my dear fellow,' he told him softly. 'You know that as well as I do.'

'No, damn you, I don't know!' Luke exploded. 'I don't know anything. I want you to tell me.'

In the background Sister gave a gasp of surprise, and Miles Channon's eyes met those of his colleague and he suddenly understood. For in front of him stood not one of his peers, a man brilliant in his own field of medicine, who had done enough neurology in his pre-clinical, clinical and post-registration days to know that an extra-dural haemorrhage carried an extremely variable prognosis.

No, here stood a man, stricken with grief, helpless and bereft without the woman he loved. And desolated by his unacknowledged fear that that woman might shortly die in the operating theatre.

Miles Channon had been a consultant neurosurgeon for almost fifteen years, the brightest star of his generation, but that afternoon he learned as basic a lesson in human psychology as any he had done as a twenty-year-old.

He cleared his throat again. 'The odds——' He stopped and tried again. 'Her chances of survival are no more than fifty-fifty,' he said, wishing he didn't feel so impotent, wishing that there was some way of softening the blow. 'I needn't tell you about the mysteries of the human brain, or of the mind itself, Luke. I want you to go in to her and to talk to her before she goes down to theatre.' The wise eyes were infinitely kind. 'We've both been doctors long enough to have seen miracles worked. Sister will take you to her now.' He put his hand on the younger man's arm.

'I shall do the best I can, and you must pray. That's all we can do.'

Luke nodded. 'Thank you, Miles.' He turned and followed Sister.

She hesitated outside the door of the cubicle, her hand on the handle. 'You know she's had her head shaved?' she asked.

He nodded again. 'Thank you, Sister. I'll go in now.'

Sister spoke to the nurse. 'You can leave Dr Hayward in here alone for five minutes. Those are Mr Channon's instructions.'

They both left the room and Luke was alone

with Claire.

She lay on the bed, her face as white as the sheet. He was aware that everything in the room seemed white—so strange and surreal, like a film set.

He walked over to her and sat down next to her. She had a drip connected to her arm, and wore a thin white hospital gown. She looked so fragile that he wanted to pick her up and cradle her in his arms. But he was so afraid lest the deadly clot move that he contented himself with gripping on to her hand.

She gave a great sighing breath and he looked at her face properly. He realised that she was not simply white, but that her skin had the translucency of wax—two dark wings of eyelashes on cold cheeks the only contrast.

The head had been partially shaved, the bright curls removed from the forehead and the middle crown. She looked so small and so alone, like a pure and ghostly nun asleep on the bed. With a tortured heart Luke thought that he had never loved her as much as he did that minute.

He began to speak to her. 'Don't leave me, Claire. Oh, my darling, please don't leave me!' He leant forward so that he was speaking into her ear. 'I've been an indecisive fool, I know that. My life means nothing without you. I want you, Claire. I want to marry you and spend the rest of my life with you. And have children—if you want them.'

He stopped for a moment and began to caress the cold, lifeless hand. 'And so you see, my darling, you've got to go down and have this silly operation, and you've got to get better as quickly as possible, because I'm taking you up to Scotland as my wife.

'You've got to understand that I love you so much. You've got to understand that, my darling Claire.'

He bent to kiss her hand, his voice breaking down, and Sister, who was opening the door, hastily dismissed the staff nurse who was close behind, with a brusqueness which was most uncharacteristic.

But the last thing she wanted was one of her nurses reporting the sight of Dr Hayward, his head in his hands, sobbing as though his heart would break.

CHAPTER SEVENTEEN

THEY allowed him to watch as they lifted Claire on to the theatre trolley, and even to accompany her to the operating theatre. As well as a nurse, she had the anaesthetic Registrar and the neuro-surgical Registrar watching her carefully as the lift rode down in silence to the operating suite.

A grim-faced Theatre Sister, wearing the lurid green dress, was waiting by the lift doors. Someone must have told them about Luke, since no one questioned his presence. He stood back awkwardly and would have followed the trolley automatically, like a sleepwalker, had the anaesthetist not barred him firmly.

'I'm sorry, Luke,' he said, a hand on his arm. 'I really can't let you come in. It's best you don't watch—you know that. We'll let you know the moment there's any news. Why don't you go and wait in Stephanie's office and one of the nurses will bring you a cup of coffee.'

Luke nodded dumbly and walked along to Stephanie Troutbeck's office. He shivered. The room felt cold, yet he knew that could not be so; theatres were kept at a constant temperature. He was beginning to show signs of shock, he thought dispassionately.

The minutes ticked by with an excruciating slowness. He tried to pray. He had not offered a prayer up since as a young boy he had lain terrified beneath the bedclothes, trying to drown the shouts and bangings of his parents, locked in their nightly combat, praying that Mummy would not go away. When that prayer had gone unanswered he had somehow got out of the habit of praying. Strange that he should think about that now.

A cup of coffee was brought to him by a serious-looking, nervous young nurse, treading as carefully as if she were dealing with the newly bereaved.

He allowed it to cool and then drank it off in a draught, his body protesting that he had taken nothing since breakfast. They had loaded it with a disproportionate amount of sugar, and he winced slightly, but it flooded welcomingly into his stomach, warm and sickly.

He remembered the cup of tea which had lain untouched on the office desk in Casualty, and how he had taken Claire to the canteen for another, then watched surreptitiously while she drank it, seeing the roses bloom again on her cheeks.

What would he do? How would he cope, if she didn't make it? He wanted to shout 'No!' at the top of his voice, to bang his fists on the desk—to tear at something. But of course he couldn't. And he wouldn't think about the worst outcome, because he had to remain strong—for her sake.

He wondered whether her mother was on her way. He knew that theirs was not a close relationship, Claire had told him that. It was another of their common bonds. But Claire had had no brothers or sisters to share the disruption and the heartbreak of divorce. At least he had grown close to Claude—a bond forged not out of blood but out of survival.

His exacting stepbrother had rung him up to express his approval of *'la belle* Claire.' How he would despise Luke's fear of commitment, which had manifested itself in that pathetic letter.

There was a sound of footsteps swiftly approaching and in the doorway stood John Fox, the anaesthetist.

Luke sprang to his feet, trying to gauge the news from the expression on the other's face, but it was professionally neutral—it gave nothing away.

'What's happened? How is she?' he demanded.

'The news is good—so far, Luke. As soon as the Burr holes were drilled, we noticed a drop in blood pressure and a corresponding rise in the pulse rate.'

Luke's face broke into a smile, but the other man shook his head.

'She's still in a coma, Luke.' He paused for a moment to let the full impact of his words sink in. 'There may be brain damage, it's too early to say. We shan't know until she wakes up.'

If she wakes up, he thought, but he didn't say it.

Luke clenched his fists. He must think positively. He was going to get Claire through this.

'Where is she now?' he asked in a calm voice, which he hardly recognised as his own.

'We're moving her straight round to Intensive Care. Would you like to come with me now?'

He nodded, his feet taking him to a ward where he'd been thousands of times as a doctor—to help in a crisis, to perform routine tests. And sometimes to help save a life.

And other times? He refused to think about the other times, to dwell even for a moment on the spectre of death which haunted this high-powered ward, with its terrifying array of machines and its highly qualified staff—watching, watching, every second of every day.

And yet now, as he passed ventilators, seeing them rising and falling and hearing their monotonous swishing sound, he felt as frightened and inexperienced as a first-year student.

John Fox led him into Claire's cubicle. Her head was now completely bandaged so that she looked even more like a nun. She lay as still and as pale as before. Was it wishful thinking, though, or did her breathing seem less laboured, less deep and harsh?

Luke gripped her hand again. 'You're doing just fine, my darling,' he told her. 'And now I'm going out for a little while. I'll be back for when you wake up.' He bent and touched his lips to hers.

He was met at the door by a small, dark girl who stopped him and said, 'Hello, Luke—I'm Mary. Do you remember, we met once, briefly?'

He managed a half smile. So this was the girl who had rung him in Glasgow, the girl who had sounded as though she despised him.

They spoke for a moment outside the cubicle, in soft tones, as though afraid Claire might overhear.

'I hear she's come through the first test,' said Mary, looking up at him with candid eyes. 'I feel I owe you an apology for the way I spoke to you on the phone earlier. I shouldn't have said what I did, but I was upset.'

Luke shook his head. 'No, you were right to say what you did. But it's important for me that you know I'm not here solely because Claire has had surgery. I'd decided to try and some way ask her to forget that I'd ever written the letter, before you phoned me.'

She nodded, recoiling slightly from the naked pain in his eyes.

'I can't help thinking,' it took a monumental effort to stop his voice from breaking as he voiced his darkest fear, 'that if I hadn't written that damn stupid letter, then she wouldn't be lying there like that.'

Now it was Mary's turn to disagree. 'You know you can't say that. No one knows what caused the accident—you can't hold yourself responsible and Claire wouldn't want you to.'

Luke nodded miserably. 'Will you stay with her until I get back?'

'Yes, of course I will.' She didn't ask where he was going, but he probably wouldn't have told her anyway, she thought as she watched him hurry away.

He took a taxi to Regent's Park Road, and crept into the church there, the one opposite the Zoo itself. The words he offered up silently made little sense to him, except the enduring wish that he would give his life in place of Claire's.

Emerging into the brightness of the late September sunshine, he blinked and walked up to her flat, crunching through the fallen leaves, and stood there just staring at the building, until he realised that he must go back to her.

He felt a childish need to buy her something, as if to reassure himself that she was still alive, but the only flower shop he could find was closed.

He saw a black cab approaching on the opposite side of the road, its bright yellow light welcoming, and he hailed it. As he waited for it to manoeuvre a three-point turn, his eye caught sight of a handwritten notice in the window of a shop behind him. Incredulously he read it, and, motioning to the cabby to wait, pushed the door open and stepped inside.

When Claire awoke she thought she must be dreaming. The first thing that she saw was the grey-green eyes she knew so well, so tender and soft and loving.

'Hello, darling,' was all Luke said, and hazily she realised that he could say no more than that, that his cheek was wet on her hand.

'Hello, Luke.'

He kissed her hand, over and over again, with gratitude. He knew that they would do their tests, that they would ask her all kinds of questions to check her mental state—but the way she looked at him, the way she said those two precious words, told him at once that she was going to be all right. Everything was going to be all right.

He waited patiently. He had all the time in the world now and he didn't want to rush her.

Claire's gaze flicked round the room, as if getting her bearings—and then stopped. For there, incongruously, hanging up on the other side of the drip stand, hung a beautiful dress—in floating layers of the palest pink tulle, the hem exquisitely embroidered with garlands of flowers.

'My dress!' She gave him a delighted smile, and then a puzzled expression as she remembered. It nagged at her mind. 'How——?' but Luke's finger was on her lips and he was shushing her.

'Your wedding dress,' he corrected her. 'If you'll have me.'

A nurse standing at the end of the bed blushed and hastily began writing on a chart. A public proposal, no less—just wait until she told the others!

John Fox, busily injecting a drug into the intravenous infusion, hid a smile.

The tiniest frown appeared. 'But I thought . . .'

There was a lilt to Claire's voice, and he could have sworn that she was teasing him—but he must be mistaken, she would still be groggy and confused.

Perhaps he should have waited until they were alone, but he didn't care. He had nearly lost her and he was never going to waste another second with her.

He leaned closer. 'Can you remember? You had a nasty crack on the skull—you nearly didn't make it. You've had an operation.' He gently lifted her fingers and ran them along the bandage that framed her forehead.

'I told you a lot of things while you were asleep. Did you hear any of them?'

There was a glint in her eyes.

'Can you remember any of them? I asked you to marry me.'

There was the most wonderful feeling of inevitability as their eyes locked. Sleepy as she was, she felt secure. Secure in his love. Secure for ever.

'Will you marry me, Claire?'

The anaesthetist frowned, a full syringe in his hand, about to inject something into the giving set.

'Don't tire her out, Luke,' he warned as he bent over her arm.

Claire flashed him a smile. 'Oh, do, Luke. Tire me out all you like!'

The nurse at the end of the bed now bristled indignantly. Honestly, only just out of a coma and the things she was saying! Just wait until they heard about *this* in the canteen!

'You still haven't answered my question,' whispered Luke, so that only Claire could hear.

The smile was brief, she could feel the drug beginning to take effect. 'You know the answer, don't you?'

And of course he did.

CHAPTER EIGHTEEN

IT HAD BEEN a boiling hot day for June, both north and south of the Border, and it came at the end of a fortnight which had broken all records, according to the excited commentaries of the weather men. England had lost another Test Match, grass was parched and ice-cream sales everywhere had soared.

But by nine o'clock, the heat was beginning to fade in a shimmering sunset, and Luke and Claire sat on their balcony, sipping iced wine with soda.

'Mmm—sheer bliss!' She slipped off her sandals and wriggled her toes luxuriously, then leaned back lazily against the basket chair.

Nothing remained of the operation now, except for a tiny ridge of scar tissue which she could just feel with her fingertip. And, naturally, the memory.

It had been worst for Luke really, she thought, as she gazed at him fondly, his golden-brown head bent over a textbook. He looked up to see her expression, and smiled.

'Darling, will you please stop looking at me like that? You're tempting me again, and I *must* read this damn textbook!'

'OK! OK!' She held her hands up in mock submission and walked over to the iron railing and rested her elbows. In the distance she could see misty hills, blue hills becoming bluer as they merged into the darkening sky.

She had remembered nothing beyond getting on her bicycle that morning and setting off for work. The van driver, who had come to visit her in hospital, overjoyed at her complete recovery, had told her that someone reported hearing the loud bang of a car backfiring, and perhaps it had been that which had distracted her.

And in the local paper, an old woman claimed to have seen a cat run wildly across the road, swerving in front of Claire's bike.

She was never to know the full story. Obviously, she hadn't been concentrating. When she had left hospital, and was preparing to join Luke, they had both had a few days of sheer terror, the reality of her lucky escape at last sinking in properly. It was then that Claire began to understand what it must have been like for those who had been waiting—the impotent torment Luke had endured.

He had made her promise never to ride the bicycle again, which was stupid really, because she would never, ever ride carelessly again, but she agreed to do it, partly because she couldn't bear to see his worried face every time she left the house.

After the euphoria of his proposal, and her acceptance, she had got cold feet, convinced that he was doing so only out of a distorted sense of duty. But as he told her on their wedding night, proving otherwise had been the most enjoyable project of his entire life!

She had formally introduced him to Simon and had

discovered how he had jumped to the wrong conclusion when he had telephoned on the afternoon of their engagement. And he had told her about the twisting black jealousy, the fear of rejection, of being cuckolded as his father had been. She was going to spend the rest of her life showing him how much she loved him.

In April, they had gone to Paris, to attend Jilly and Claude's wedding. There Claire had met Luke's mother Sara—a tall, elegant woman dressed impeccably in silk and pearls, who had stared coldly at Claire.

She had tried her best, she really had, but in the end she had given up. If mother and son were like polite strangers, then how could she fare any better? But she had got on tolerably well with Jean-Claude, Sara's husband—and when she and Luke were leaving for the airport, she had given them their Glasgow address and asked them to visit at any time. Perhaps time might heal the rift, she thought.

Their own wedding had been on Christmas Eve, a quiet and simple service in the church where Luke had gone that day to pray. Claire's mother and Ian McGregor had flown over from New Zealand to stay with her while she recovered, and had stayed on for the wedding.

Luke had been his strong, charming, loving self and she had seen her mother won over by him.

'I felt that you were too young,' she told Claire one day, as they were packing up her books for the move. 'But now that I've met him, I'm perfectly happy. You're a lucky girl, Claire—he's a man in a million.'

'I know,' Claire had replied softly, and had hugged her mother. The years of mother-daughter conflict and bickering had been dissolved. Her illness had had its positive aspects, and life had become so precious and valued to those around her, who had gazed on death.

She had been advised by her doctors to take things easy for a while. Mrs Haynes had told her that she should re-apply to start her training in Glasgow, when she felt well enough. She could probably get a place at the Western General. But Claire was no longer sure if she wanted the long hours of nursing to separate them again.

The wedding was at four and it was already dark by the time she entered the church, a huge spray of fragrant pink and white roses her bouquet. She wore the dress which Luke had found again for her. By some incredible stroke of fate, the dress had been handed in to the shop just a few days before her accident. It had lain forgotten, gathering dust in the bedroom of the boy on the bicycle, who had rung for the ambulance that day on Primrose Hill. His mother had discovered it and handed it in to the shop where Claire had bought it.

Luke told her that when he saw it, it was like a sign from heaven, a good omen—and it made him certain that she would recover.

The church was lit entirely by candles, and as the organ swelled into song, she had felt tears prick her eyes.

As they left the church, the first snowflakes of winter began to fall, brushing their cheeks, and Luke's arm rested protectively around her shoulders as they stood, straining their ears to hear the sound of carol singers, a few streets away.

'I want you to know that this is the happiest moment of my life,' he had said to her, his lips on her cheek.

'Mine too,' Claire had murmured, her heart feeling so full that she felt it would burst.

Six months ago, six gloriously happy months. How they had flown! she thought as she turned and walked back to her chair. Night had claimed the city for her own. The balcony was lit by floodlight, and she caught the musky scent of geraniums from her windowbox on the air.

Luke glanced up as she sat down and the green-grey eyes narrowed appreciatively. He put the textbook on the table and came and sat by her feet.

'I thought you were supposed to be studying,' she reprimanded him softly.

'I am. I'm studying my wife. You look lovely tonight,' he observed.

'Thank you.' Her hands lay demurely in her lap, and a tendril of hair brushed against her cheek. The hair had almost completely grown back, as glossy and as bright and as curly as before.

'And very pleased with yourself, I must say.'

'Do I?' she smiled mischievously.

'Why is that, then?' he enquired lazily, massaging an ankle. There was no reply, and when he looked up he saw a face bursting with love and pride.

'Can't you guess?' she asked him. 'Oh, darling, can't you guess?'

and then 'Yes' and 'Yes', nodding her head and laughing, 'Yes, it's really true!' as he stared at her incredulously. And then he took her in his arms and gazed at her with such a look of wonderment that she felt she would cry.

'It's due at the end of January,' she told him, as he hugged her to him, stroking her hair and murmuring 'sweetheart' and 'darling' over and over again, and the way he said it made her melt with longing.

And later, as they lay in bed, Claire realised that Luke had been watching her silently, and she caressed his shoulder and asked him what he was thinking.

He shook his head a little. 'When you lay there so ill, and we didn't know if you'd live or die, with your head shaved—you looked so vulnerable, and I thought that I could never love you as much as I did at that moment.

'Then, as we came out of the church on our wedding day, I thought much the same thing.' He began to stroke her hair.

'And?'

'Well, earlier, when you told me about the baby—well, I thought it again, only more so.'

Claire was grinning with delight now. 'And what's wrong with that?'

He smiled at her. 'Nothing. Nothing at all. It's just that it's so good, and it keeps getting better, and sometimes I wonder if it's all one long dream.'

She pulled the duvet over them and bent her face to his.

'If this is a dream,' she whispered, 'may we never wake up.'